TEEN RIGHTS AND FREEDOMS

I Disabilities

Teen Rights and Freedoms

I Disabilities

David Haugen and Susan Musser
Book Editors

GREENHAVEN PRESS
A part of Gale, Cengage Learning

**SCHOOL OF EDUCATION
CURRICULUM LABORATORY
UM-DEARBORN**

GALE
CENGAGE Learning·

Detroit • New York • San Francisco • New Haven, Conn • Waterville, Maine • London

Elizabeth Des Chenes, *Director, Content Strategy*
Cynthia Sanner, *Publisher*
Douglas Dentino, *Manager, New Product*

Articles in Greenhaven Press anthologies are often edited for length to meet page requirements. In addition, original titles of these works are changed to clearly present the main thesis and to explicitly indicate the author's opinion. Every effort is made to ensure the Greenhaven Press accurately reflects the original intent of the authors. Every effort has been made to trace the owners of copyrighted material.

Cover Image © Stokkete/Shutterstock.com

LIBRARY OF CONGRESS CATALOGING-IN-PUBLICATION DATA

Disabilities / David Haugen and Susan Musser, book editors.
   pages cm. -- (Teen rights and freedoms)
   Includes bibliographical references and index.
   ISBN 978-0-7377-6995-1 (hardcover)
   1. People with disabilities--United States. 2. People with disabilities--Legal status, laws, etc.--United States I. Haugen, David M., 1969- editor of compilation. II. Musser, Susan, editor of compilation.
HV1553.D543 2014
323.3--dc23
                                  2013036323

Printed in the United States of America
1 2 3 4 5 6 7 18 17 16 15 14

Contents

Foreword   1

Introduction   4

Chronology   7

1. **The Disability Rights Movement: An Overview**   15

    Richard K. Scotch

    A sociology professor traces the history of the disability rights movement from the late nineteenth century through the early twenty-first century.

2. **Mentally Disabled Individuals Must Receive Minimum Levels of Care Within Institutions**   29

    The Circuit Court's Decision

    Frank Minis Johnson Jr.

    In the 1971 case *Wyatt v. Stickney*, a federal judge rules that Alabama state institutions must provide a minimum level of care to their patients.

3. **Mandating Minimum Levels of Care Could Impede Care in Institutions**   41

    Charles C. Cleland and Gary V. Sluyter

    Two mental health professionals maintain that the mandated minimum levels of care established by the 1971 ruling in *Wyatt v. Stickney* could create new problems within mental health institutes, potentially hindering patient care.

4. **States Cannot Hold Individuals in an Institution if They Do Not Present a Threat to Themselves or Others**   50

    The Supreme Court's Decision

    Potter Stewart

A US Supreme Court justice delivers the unanimous ruling in the 1975 case *O'Connor v. Donaldson*. The Court found it a violation of the US Constitution for a state to confine to an institution a person who is not deemed a danger, if it is possible for that individual to exist freely in society either on his own or with help from others.

5. The Court's Ruling on Institutionalization of the Mentally Disabled Lacks Strength   56

J.L. Bernard

A psychologist maintains that the ruling in *O'Connor v. Donaldson* does not concretely define the terms "dangerous" and "treatment," thereby leaving interpretation of the ruling up to individual courts and officials, possibly lessening its impact.

6. A Man Wrongly Held in an Institution Recounts His Life and His Struggle to Be Released   66
Personal Narrative

Kenneth Donaldson

A man confined against his will for fifteen years in a mental hospital describes the conditions within the institution and his efforts to be released.

7. Individuals with Mental Disabilities Have the Right to Live in a Community Instead of an Institution   75
The Supreme Court's Decision

Ruth Bader Ginsburg

A US Supreme Court justice delivers the court's ruling in *Olmstead v. L.C. and E.W.* (1999), which states that when deemed permissible by mental health professionals, individuals have the right to participate in community placement programs instead of remaining in an institution.

8. **Students Have the Right to Receive a Free Public Education Regardless of Disability or Cost**   87
The Circuit Court's Decision

Joseph Cornelius Waddy

In *Mills v. Board of Education of the District of Columbia* (1972), a case regarding the public education of children with disabilities, a federal judge finds that public schools are required by law to provide an education for all students, including those with disabilities, and they cannot deny students an education based on the cost of provisions necessary to deliver that education.

9. **The Reauthorized IDEA Should Mandate an Equal, Integrated Education for All Children**   99

Nina Zuna and Rud Turnbull

Two advocates for disability rights argue that the Individuals with Disabilities Education Act of 1990, which provides guidelines for the education of children with disabilities, should be more inclusive and mandate integrated educational settings to provide equal educational opportunities for all children in public schools.

10. **The Mother of a Student with Learning Disabilities Calls for More Integrated Learning Environments**   109
Personal Narrative

Leigh M. O'Brien

A woman who has a young daughter with a developmental disability details her daughter's struggles as well as her own and describes how being labeled "a child with special needs" by the education system and society makes it more difficult for her daughter to learn and participate in society.

11. **Students with Disabilities Cannot Be Moved from Their Educational Placement Without Proper Evaluation**　　　117
The Supreme Court's Decision

William J. Brennan

A US Supreme Court justice delivers the opinion of the court in *Honig v. Doe* (1988), which states that a child with a disability cannot be removed from his placement in a class based on behavior resulting from his disability without expert evaluation of the situation or parental consent.

12. **Schools Must Appropriately Discipline Students with Disabilities Within the Mandated Guidelines**　　128

Mitchell L. Yell

A special education academic argues that discipline is a necessary condition for a productive educational environment. He contends that federal legislation and court rulings create a body of law that, while sometimes confusing, can be used by educators to construct meaningful disciplinary guidelines and procedures that benefit all students without violating their rights.

13. **A Federally Funded Education Program Can Deny Admittance to a Disabled Individual Based on an Inability to Meet All Program Requirements**　　139
The Supreme Court's Decision

Lewis F. Powell

A US Supreme Court justice delivers the court's unanimous ruling in *Southeastern Community College v. Davis* (1979), which states that a federally funded school is not required by law to make significant modifications to its program of study to accommodate individuals with a disability who would otherwise be unable to satisfactorily complete the tasks required of them.

14. **The Americans with Disabilities Act Will Advance Civil Rights for Disabled Americans** 148

Dick Thornburgh

A US attorney general, writing in 1990, asserts that the Americans with Disabilities Act of 1990 will overcome the failures of previous disability rights legislation.

15. **A Young Adult Examines the Impact of Personal Assistance Services on Her Life** 159
Personal Narrative

Sascha Bittner

An eighteen-year-old woman describes the ways in which her use of personal assistance services to complete certain daily tasks has both allowed and limited her participation in activities easily manageable for individuals without disabilities.

16. **A Man Disabled as a Child Reflects on the Importance of the Americans with Disabilities Act on His Life** 166
Personal Narrative

Adrian Villalobos

A man who was badly injured as an eight-year-old child and permanently confined to a wheelchair describes how the Americans with Disabilities Act of 1990 made it easier for him to attend school and participate in extracurricular activities.

Organizations to Contact 173
For Further Reading 178
Index 181

Foreword

"In the truest sense freedom cannot be bestowed, it must be achieved."
Franklin D. Roosevelt,
September 16, 1936

The notion of children and teens having rights is a relatively recent development. Early in American history, the head of the household—nearly always the father—exercised complete control over the children in the family. Children were legally considered to be the property of their parents. Over time, this view changed, as society began to acknowledge that children have rights independent of their parents, and that the law should protect young people from exploitation. By the early twentieth century, more and more social reformers focused on the welfare of children, and over the ensuing decades advocates worked to protect them from harm in the workplace, to secure public education for all, and to guarantee fair treatment for youths in the criminal justice system. Throughout the twentieth century, rights for children and teens—and restrictions on those rights—were established by Congress and reinforced by the courts. Today's courts are still defining and clarifying the rights and freedoms of young people, sometimes expanding those rights and sometimes limiting them. Some teen rights are outside the scope of public law and remain in the realm of the family, while still others are determined by school policies.

Each volume in the Teen Rights and Freedoms series focuses on a different right or freedom and offers an anthology of key essays and articles on that right or freedom and the responsibilities that come with it. Material within each volume is drawn from a diverse selection of primary and secondary sources— journals, magazines, newspapers, nonfiction books, organization newsletters, position papers, speeches, and government documents, with a particular emphasis on Supreme Court and lower court decisions. Volumes also include first-person narratives from young people and others involved in teen rights issues, such as parents and educators. The material is selected and arranged to highlight all the major social and legal controversies relating to the right or freedom under discussion. Each selection is preceded by an introduction that provides context and background. In many cases, the essays point to the difference between adult and teen rights, and why this difference exists.

Many of the volumes cover rights guaranteed under the Bill of Rights and how these rights are interpreted and protected in regard to children and teens, including freedom of speech, freedom of the press, due process, and religious rights. The scope of the series also encompasses rights or freedoms, whether real or perceived, relating to the school environment, such as electronic devices, dress, Internet policies, and privacy. Some volumes focus on the home environment, including topics such as parental control and sexuality.

Numerous features are included in each volume of Teen Rights and Freedoms:

- An annotated **table of contents** provides a brief summary of each essay in the volume and highlights court decisions and personal narratives.
- An **introduction** specific to the volume topic gives context for the right or freedom and its impact on daily life.
- A brief **chronology** offers important dates associated with the right or freedom, including landmark court cases.
- **Primary sources**—including personal narratives and court decisions—are among the varied selections in the anthology.
- **Illustrations**—including photographs, charts, graphs, tables, statistics, and maps—are closely tied to the text and chosen to help readers understand key points or concepts.

- An annotated list of **organizations to contact** presents sources of additional information on the topic.
- A **for further reading** section offers a bibliography of books, periodical articles, and Internet sources for further research.
- A comprehensive subject **index** provides access to key people, places, events, and subjects cited in the text.

Each volume of Teen Rights and Freedoms delves deeply into the issues most relevant to the lives of teens: their own rights, freedoms, and responsibilities. With the help of this series, students and other readers can explore from many angles the evolution and current expression of rights both historic and contemporary.

Introduction

Henry Miles Frost is a teenager with autism. He has a service dog, and he communicates using an iPad that translates his typed words into speech. Frost lives in Tampa, Florida, where the Hillsborough County school district wanted him to go to a special school for kids with special needs, but Frost disagreed. In 2012 Frost posted a picture of himself and his service dog on Facebook. In the picture Frost holds a handmade sign that reads, "The Civil Rights Act of 1964 granted equal rights to all people. I am a person. I want these rights." Frost's picture went viral, drawing thousands of supporters who insisted that Frost be allowed to attend the local "regular" school, Wilson Middle School, with his friends and peers.

Frost's situation highlights a longstanding issue: how children with disabilities are treated in schools in the United States. Parents and their children often prefer to choose their school, but many state and local governments have laws that define how best to educate students with special needs, and that may mean that the local school district decides where these students can attend classes to receive the attention they need. Hillsborough County School Board Chairwoman Candy Olson says, "It's difficult to tell a parent they can't send their child to the school of their choice, but the district only does so when they believe the student would be better-served or safer at a different school." Opponents believe it is up to school districts to prove why kids with special needs cannot attend a regular school, often called a mainstream school. The districts often counter such claims by saying that parents must show that their children can handle a mainstream workload, something not all children with disabilities can do. In addition, the districts insist that school budgets cannot support special teachers for every school, so specially created schools that serve kids with disabilities are more cost effective. Sometimes, even if parents succeed in sending their special-needs child to a regular school, they find that mainstream classes are not the best option. Ann Siegel, an attorney with Disability Rights Florida—the group handling Frost's dispute with the school district as well as hundreds of others in the region—claims the situations never resolve themselves perfectly for all involved. "Even when you win, you've lost time. And you've tainted a relationship with the school district," she says.

In November 2012 Frost was granted the right to attend Wilson Middle School—a scant 175 yards from his home—rather than the farther-away special-needs school. Autism Rights Watch, an advocacy organization that believes kids with autism should be mainstreamed, announced, "Henry's case proved that, together, we can defeat segregation in the school system." Of course, not all campaigns achieve such results. Parents, students, and school boards perpetually are caught up in rules that try to define where students with disabilities will get the best education and how their needs can be met by balancing students' rights with the educational resources available.

Frost's battle to attend a mainstream school is an issue specifically concerning the rights of young people with disabilities. However, many other battles for disability rights have been waged on a broader scale. For instance, throughout the twentieth century, disabled individuals and their advocates have countered discrimination in the workplace, fought for access to public facilities, and demanded that public transportation facilitate the needs of people with disabilities. In 1990 US Congress passed the Americans with Disabilities Act (ADA), a landmark piece of civil rights legislation that addressed many of the issues people with disabilities face and added other protections as well. It also outlined who can lawfully be termed "disabled" and extended protections accordingly. Opponents at the time argued that the costs of implementing the ADA would be excessive. They claimed that building ramps to public facilities and businesses, refitting city transportation with chairlifts, and accommodating other requirements under the law would tax public funds and private profits.

The US government responded by insisting that the changes could be implemented over time to ensure that the pressure on available resources would not be immediate or disruptive. The government, however, was firm in that the changes needed to occur to protect the civil rights of the disabled. When he signed the ADA into law, President George H.W. Bush remarked:

> This act is powerful in its simplicity. It will ensure that people with disabilities are given the basic guarantees for which they have worked so long and so hard: independence, freedom of choice, control of their lives, the opportunity to blend fully and equally into the rich mosaic of the American mainstream. . . . Together, we must remove the physical barriers we have created and the social barriers that we have accepted. For ours will never be a truly prosperous nation until all within it prosper.

In the early twenty-first century, the spirit of the ADA still guides the ways in which people with disabilities continue to fight to broaden access to public and private facilities and counteract discrimination in the workplace and other venues. Although Henry Frost's fight over educational rights is not addressed by the ADA, the legislation's rigid stance against segregation certainly has helped convince many that people with disabilities have the guaranteed right to demolish any barriers that keep them from being part of mainstream society.

In *Teen Rights and Freedoms: Disabilities*, authors offer opinions on the institutionalization of the disabled, the extent of the protections offered by the ADA, the restrictions on educational opportunities, and other issues related to disability rights. Together these viewpoints illustrate how far the United States has come in protecting the rights of its citizens and how far the country has yet to go in ensuring that these basic protections are not eroded or compromised.

Chronology

1918

US Congress passes the Smith-Sears Veterans Rehabilitation Act, which establishes a program of vocational rehabilitation and civil employment for disabled US military veterans.

May 2, 1927

The US Supreme Court rules in *Buck v. Bell* that sterilizing people with disabilities by force does not violate their constitutional rights. In the following fifty years more than sixty thousand disabled people were sterilized without their consent.

1943

Congress passes the Vocational Rehabilitation Amendments, also known as the LaFollette-Barden Act, which adds physical rehabilitation to federally funded vocational rehabilitation programs and provides funding for certain health-care services.

1945

Congress passes House Joint Resolution 23, establishing the first week in October as National Employ the Physically Handicapped Week. In 1988 Congress expands the commemoration to a month, renaming it National Disability Employment Awareness Month.

1946

Passage of the Hill-Burton Act offers federal grants to states for the purpose of constructing institutions and facilities for people with disabilities.

May 17, 1954

In *Brown v. Board of Education* the Supreme Court rules that segregated schools are unconstitutional. This decision ignites the national civil rights movement.

1955

The President's Committee on National Employ the Physically Handicapped Week becomes the permanent federal organization known as the President's Committee on Employment of the Physically Handicapped.

1963

Federal grants become available to establish new public and private nonprofit community mental health centers with the passage of the Mental Retardation Facilities and Community Health Centers Construction Act.

August 12, 1968

Congress passes the Architectural Barriers Act, which mandates that all federally funded buildings must be accessible to all physically handicapped persons.

March 12, 1971

The District Court of Alabama rules in *Wyatt v. Stickney* that patients in state mental institutions have a right to individual treatment. Not providing this treatment violates patients' due process rights.

May 5, 1972

In *PARC v. Pennsylvania* the US District Court in eastern Pennsylvania finds the laws allowing the exclusion of students with disabilities from public schools to be unconstitutional.

August 1, 1972

In *Mills v. Board of Education of the District of Columbia* the Washington, DC, District Court rules that children with disabilities must be provided a free, appropriate public education and cannot be excluded from school on the basis of their disability.

September 26, 1973

Congress passes the Rehabilitation Act, which contains sections that specifically outlaw discrimination against people with disabilities in federally funded programs and services.

June 26, 1975

The Supreme Court rules in *O'Connor v. Donaldson* that it is unconstitutional for a state to hold an individual in an institution if that person is not dangerous and is able to live safely in society on his or her own or with assistance from family and friends.

November 29, 1975

US President Gerald Ford signs the Education for All Handicapped Children Act into law. The legislation calls for a free, appropriate public education in the least restrictive setting for all children in the United States, regardless of disability.

January 18, 1977 The US Court of Appeals for the Seventh Circuit rules in *Lloyd v. Regional Transportation Authority* that Section 504 of the Rehabilitation Act of 1973 grants individuals the right to sue public transit authorities that do not provide accessible service.

May 5, 1977 The US Court of Appeals for the Fifth Circuit undermines the ruling in *Lloyd v. Regional Transportation Authority* in its decision for *Snowden v. Birmingham-Jefferson County Transit Authority*, finding that transportation authorities are only required to provide access to individuals with disabilities who do not use wheelchairs.

June 11, 1979 The Supreme Court decides in *Southeastern Community College v. Davis* that a federally funded college program is not required to admit or make accommodations for a student who is not able to fulfill all the requirements of the program as a result of his or her disability.

July 5, 1984 In *Irving Independent School District v. Tatro* the Supreme Court finds that school districts are required to perform services for students with disabilities that allow those students to attend public schools; students cannot be excluded from public schools because they need these services.

April 23, 1985   The Supreme Court rules in *Cleburne v. Cleburne Living Center* that zoning laws cannot be used to justify the prohibition of the construction of a group home for individuals with disabilities in a residential area just because the intended residents are individuals with disabilities.

April 29, 1985   The Supreme Court rules in *Burlington School Committee v. Department of Education* that schools are responsible for the cost of students with disabilities enrolling in a private school during litigation, if that placement is deemed necessary to provide the students with an education in the least restrictive environment.

January 20, 1988   In *Honig v. Doe* the Supreme Court rules that children with disabilities must be allowed to remain in their educational placement setting as outlined in their Individualized Education Program, unless a due process hearing is conducted to determine appropriate removal.

July 26, 1990   US President George H.W. Bush signs the Americans with Disabilities Act into law. It becomes the most comprehensive disability rights law in US history.

October 30, 1990   US President George H.W. Bush signs the Individuals with Disabilities

Education Act into law; it is an amended and renamed version of the Education for All Handicapped Children Act of 1975.

January 4, 1994 The US Court of Appeals for the Ninth Circuit determines in *Sacramento City School District v. Holland* that children with disabilities have the right to receive their public education alongside children without disabilities.

June 15, 1998 In *Pennsylvania Department of Corrections v. Yeskey* the Supreme Court rules that state prisons must comply with the Americans with Disabilities Act of 1990.

June 25, 1998 In *Bragdon v. Abbott* the Supreme Court finds that reproduction can be defined as a major life activity and can qualify an individual for protection under the Americans with Disabilities Act of 1990.

February 22, 1999 The Supreme Court delivers rulings in three cases known as the *Sutton* trilogy. In each of these cases—*Sutton v. United Airlines*, *Murphy v. United Parcel Service*, and *Albertsons, Inc. v. Kirkingburg*—the court finds that conditions that do not substantially limit a major life activity or could be corrected easily do not qualify as disabilities under the Americans with Disabilities Act of 1990.

June 22, 1999   In *Olmsted v. L.C. and E.W.* the Supreme Court determines that individuals with disabilities must be treated in a community setting if it meets their needs and if the individual prefers the community setting to an institutional one.

May 29, 2001   The Supreme Court rules in *PGA Tour, Inc. v. Martin* that, under the Americans with Disabilities Act of 1990, the Professional Golfers' Association (PGA) of America cannot deny Casey Martin, a golfer with a disability, the option of riding in a golf cart between shots because it would not significantly affect the game.

June 20, 2002   The Supreme Court rules in *Atkins v. Virginia* that executing individuals who are mentally handicapped violates the Eighth Amendment, which prohibits cruel and unusual punishment.

May 17, 2004   The Supreme Court finds in *Tennessee v. Lane* that by allowing individuals to sue states for monetary damages because they are unable to access services as a result of their disability, Congress did not violate the sovereign immunity doctrine of the Eleventh Amendment.

September 25, 2008   President George W. Bush signs the ADA Amendments Act into law. The new law broadens the Americans with

Disabilities Act of 1990 by expanding
the disabilities covered and more
specifically defining what qualifies
as a disability under the law.

1

> *"For over a century, but particularly in the past forty years, Americans with disabilities have engaged in social and political collective action to shape their social role and legal treatment."*

The Disability Rights Movement: An Overview

Richard K. Scotch

In the following viewpoint, Richard K. Scotch discusses the history of the disability rights movement. According to Scotch, one of the greatest strengths of the movement is its autonomy, which began in the late nineteenth century with advocacy groups formed by deaf and blind individuals and continued with both the disabled veterans groups that formed following World War II and the groups established on college campuses by students with disabilities in the 1960s and 1970s. Scotch credits all of these groups with contributing important gains to the development of disability rights within the United States, a collective effort that ultimately led to the passage of the Americans with Disabilities Act (ADA) in 1990. While he concedes that this legislation has not completely fulfilled the promise of equal rights for those with disabilities, Scotch contends that it provides the fundamentals for future improvements. Richard K. Scotch is a sociology, public policy, and

Richard K. Scotch, "Nothing About Us Without Us: Disability Rights in America," *Organization of American Historians Magazine of History,* vol. 23, no. 3, July 2009, pp. 17–22.

political economy professor at the University of Texas at Dallas. He previously served as president of the Society for Disability Studies and authored the book From Good Will to Civil Rights: Transforming Federal Disability.

The concept of legal rights for people with disabilities is rooted in the long established American ideals of autonomy and self-determination. Application of these ideals to disabled people, however, is relatively new. In early American history, individuals with disabilities were barely discernible as a separate group. Many people had a variety of impairments, but they were generally an integral and unremarkable part of the larger community in which they lived. In the nineteenth and much of the twentieth century, having a disability came to be seen as a tragically defining characteristic that would and should keep people apart. Disabled people were perceived as a dependent, marginal, and often morally questionable minority who required special care but were best kept out of public life through a combination of charity and social exclusion. Largely as a result of political advocacy by groups of disabled Americans, disability has come to be perceived in recent decades as the intersection of biological attributes, cultural constructs, and social opportunities, in which the lives of people with disabilities are shaped by the presence or absence of opportunities and accommodations to their impairments. In this latter formulation, people with disabilities can be considered to have agency, to have the ability to shape their own lives.

While these varying perspectives on disability were formed by broad historical currents and social forces, they have also been the result of specific political circumstances, and brought about especially by the efforts of people with disabilities who acted individually and particularly in concert to insist that they control their own lives and be accepted in the life of the larger society. For over a century, but particularly in the past forty years, Americans with disabilities have engaged in social and political collective action to shape their social role and legal treatment. Sometimes this action has focused on the promotion of community among people like themselves, as in the case of disabled veterans or single disability groups such as the blind or the deaf. Political advocacy by groups of the disabled, organized and led by disabled people themselves, has helped to support their independence and self-determination by striking down obstacles to participation and challenging exclusionary attitudes, policies, and physical and institutional barriers. In this essay, I provide a historical overview of self-advocacy by Americans with disabilities and of their achievements in attaining political and legal rights and cultural legitimacy and acceptance.

Self-Advocacy Begins

Perhaps the oldest American disability self-advocacy organization is the National Association of the Deaf (NAD), which was founded in 1880 in Cincinnati, Ohio. NAD came to represent the community of people who were culturally deaf and focused in particular on the education of Deaf children. At NAD's first national convention, chair Edward Booth stated that "We have interests peculiar to ourselves which can be taken care of by ourselves." NAD was active in promoting American Sign Language and rejecting oral communication methods favored by many non-Deaf educators. It also worked to expand employment opportunities for deaf workers, particularly in the public sector.

While organizations of the deaf and, to a lesser extent, the blind were formed in the nineteenth century in response to or as extensions of state schools and other impairment-specific facilities, few self-advocacy organizations, comprised of people with impairments other than blindness and deafness, developed in this period. While rates of disability were increasing, people with other impairments often remained relatively isolated.

Advocacy Groups Fight for Equal Employment Opportunities

This began to change in the early decades of the twentieth century as impairments became more common in the United States and with the development of "common social space," in which people with disabilities might congregate, including rehabilitation facilities and hospitals. Disabled workers were recruited to work in the expanding number of sheltered workshops promoted by federal procurement opportunities offered through the Fair Labor Standards Act of 1938. Meanwhile, mainstream worksites during the world wars offered expanded employment opportunities for people with disabilities, as nondisabled workers were serving in the military. Disabled veterans groups formed after World War I and World War II. Organizations of people with disabilities that were established in the early twentieth century included the National Fraternal Society of the Deaf in 1901 and the Disabled American Veterans [DAV] in 1920.

During the Great Depression of the 1930s, the League of the Physically Handicapped, a militant group of disabled job seekers, was founded in New York City with the goal of making New Deal public employment positions accessible to people with physical disabilities. Many of the League's members were the children of Jewish European immigrants and were high school graduates who had met in special education classes and subsequently at a Manhattan recreation center. In May 1935, League members held a sit-down protest at the headquarters of the Emergency Relief Bureau, demanding that workers with disabilities have access to public work relief programs. A month of protests followed, with several arrests of disabled protesters and their supporters. More protests were held in November 1935 and again in the spring of 1936, with the result that the Works Progress Administration (WPA) opened up its programs in New York City to 1,500 workers with disabilities.

A more ambitious goal of national access to jobs led League representatives to successfully seek a meeting with the WPA na-

Advocates celebrate the passage of the Americans with Disabilities Act of 1990 with US Representative Steny Hoyer (left) and US Senator Orrin Hatch (second from the left) on July 13, 1990. © Terry Ashe/Time Life Pictures/Getty Images.

tional director, Harry Hopkins, but Hopkins was unwilling to accept the proposition that the WPA discriminated against people with physical disabilities. In response, the League issued a "Thesis on Conditions of Physically Handicapped." Their thesis and its recommendations, however, were rejected by the [President Franklin D.] Roosevelt administration. By 1938, the League had dissolved without having created an institutional base for further disability advocacy. Nevertheless, the model of an informal group of friends with varying impairments uniting for political protest was to be recreated in the late 1960s and 1970s.

In 1940, Jacobus tenBroek, a law professor at the University of California Berkeley, founded the National Federation of the Blind (NFB), an advocacy organization comprised primarily of blind men and women—not their parents, friends, or sympathetic social reformers, but blind people themselves. tenBroek, who had lost his eyesight at the age of fourteen, served as the

NFB's first president and continued in that position from 1940 to 1961 and again from 1966 until his death in 1968. Under ten-Broek's leadership and that of his successors, the NFB worked for laws to allow blind people full access to the broader society through testimony at legislative hearings, lobbying and letter writing campaigns, and public protests. Some particular issues focused on by NFB were the employment opportunities for blind people beyond sheltered workshops and the promotion of local White Cane Laws that guaranteed access in public places to anyone using a white cane.

The Fight for Rights Expands

The period after the Second World War was a transitional period for disability rights. Existing disabled veterans organizations such as the DAV and newly founded groups such as the Paralyzed Veterans of America and the Blinded Veterans Association exerted influence on policymakers and a sympathetic public. Largely in response to the needs of disabled veterans, a President's Committee on National Employ the Handicapped Week was founded and ultimately became a locus for networking among a variety of disability activist organizations. Established advocacy groups for the blind and deaf expanded. The overall increase in societal wealth and broadened political support for social welfare that was a legacy of the New Deal allowed for expansion of federal social insurance programs, including those targeting people with disabilities.

One key development in post-World War II America was the growth of an energetic movement of parents of disabled children and adults, particularly the parents of individuals with intellectual disabilities, known at the time as the mentally retarded. This parents' movement sought not only to influence local schools and human service systems to offer more community services to their children but also to improve conditions and to expand services available within the growing residential institutions that housed many individuals with such conditions. Parents vigorously sought reform through lobbying and legal action, although rarely through public protests, through groups such as the National Association for Retarded Children (NARC), later called the National Association for Retarded Citizens, and finally, The Arc.

This advocacy exposed appalling conditions in many state institutions and schools and promoted the inclusion of children with disabilities in public education. It ultimately led to significant expansion of the right to universal education that culminated in the passage of the Individuals with Disabilities Education Act [IDEA] in 1974, a law that mandated a free and appropriate public education and related services regardless of impairment. However, the parents' movement also claimed unique legitimacy to speak for the interests of their disabled children, a legitimacy sometimes at odds with the disability rights goals of self-advocacy and independence. The latter goals were to be increasingly expressed through the autonomous disability rights movement that emerged in the late 1960s and early 1970s.

The Autonomous Disability Rights Movement Emerges

In 1970, a college student named Judy Heumann gathered a group of her friends and associates at Long Island University (LIU) in Brooklyn, New York, to protest her denial of teaching credentials by the New York City schools. Heumann was a polio survivor and wheelchair user. Some members of the group had met as participants in summer recreation programs for adolescents who had disabilities, while others had found each other while disabled students on the LIU campus. The informal group developed into a protest organization, Disabled in Action (DIA), which expanded from protesting the discrimination faced by Heumann to addressing local access issues in New York City and national disability polices following President [Richard M.] Nixon's vetoes of the Rehabilitation Acts of 1972 and 1973.

"Disability" Redefined

Why are disability rights so frequently overlooked as a civil rights issue by scholars and the general public? Why is there reluctance to accept disability as a form of diversity serving as reassurance of the human capacity for resourcefulness and innovation? Why is there backlash against the disability rights movement, which advanced and continues to advance the civil rights of people with disabilities? Because the disability rights movement approaches disability in a new, unfamiliar way, people may be threatened as their perception of disability tends to be through the "impairment model," rather than the "civil rights model." The former, this traditional perception, underlies the Social Security disability system in the United States with which most adults come to associate the term "disability." This view purports that because impairment causes disability, which prevents effective functioning in the world, unless one is cured, one cannot expect equality. Therefore, as the disability rights movement, which struggles for social equality of people with disabilities, redefines "disability," the movement also challenges basic social assumptions about the nature of disability.

*Doris Zames Fleischer and Frieda Zames,
"Disability Rights: The Overlooked Civil Rights
Issue," Disability Studies Quarterly, Fall 2005.*

Forming additional chapters in Philadelphia and several other eastern U.S. cities, DIA became involved in a wide range of disability rights issues, including architectural and transportation barriers, charitable fundraising telethons that promoted negative stereotypes related to impairment, and the campaigns to pass and enforce the Americans with Disabilities Act.

In the late 1960s, another informal group of college students with disabilities at the University of California Berkeley formed a social network that evolved into a key component of the disability rights movement. This group included Ed Roberts, a polio survivor who has been called the father of the movement, and other students, who first resided in the university's health clinic due to the lack of accessible housing and came to be known as the Rolling Quads. Roberts and his fellow activists left their campus and went on to found the Center for Independent Living (CIL), a model for independence, self-advocacy, and peer support programs that spread across the United States. The disability community in Berkeley and the East San Francisco Bay attracted East Coast activist Judy Heumann, who attended graduate school and became director of CIL when Roberts was appointed to be California's Commissioner of Rehabilitation by Governor Jerry Brown in 1975.

In the 1970s, local disability activist groups were founded in cities and on college campuses across the United States. Local organizing was enhanced by a growing national network of organizations of people with disabilities, first through national meetings of the President's Committee on the National Employ the Handicapped Week and later on its own through self-advocacy efforts such as the American Coalition of Citizens with Disabilities (ACCD). ACCD brought together a number of long-standing national groups representing people with specific impairments or veterans, as well as the newer, mostly local cross-disability organizations such as DIA. Other organizations that served to establish a national disability rights movement included legal advocacy centers such as the National Center on Law and the Handicapped and the Disability Rights Education and Defense Fund, modeled on the Legal Defense Fund of the NAACP [National Association for the Advancement of Colored People].

Momentum Increases

The emergence of the American disability rights movement and these focal organizations was promoted by a series of events related to the implementation of the first major civil rights provision protecting people with disabilities, Section 504 of the

Rehabilitation Act of 1973. Section 504 was modeled on Title VI of the Civil Rights Act of 1964, which prohibited discrimination on the basis of race by recipients of federal funds. It was drafted by congressional staff and passed without controversy. But its implications for establishing a federal commitment to rights of access for people with disabilities were profound—covering local schools, colleges, public transportation systems, hospitals, social service agencies, and government offices. As federal officials became aware of the potential scope of the law, implementation of the section was delayed by the [President Gerald] Ford and early [President Jimmy] Carter administrations.

Professional staff in the Office of Civil Rights had worked closely with disability advocacy organizations, including many of those mentioned in this essay, to draft regulations for Section 504. This consultation had educated movement organizations about the potential of the section, and they sought ways to force the government to put the section into effect. A lawsuit, *Cherry v. Matthews* [1976], was filed against President Ford's Secretary of Health, Education and Welfare (HEW) [F. David Matthews] with little immediate result. After expectations were raised by the election of Jimmy Carter, but then dashed by continued delays by Carter's HEW Secretary Joseph Califano, a more contentious strategy was adopted by the national network of disability activists. Protests were organized at many of the regional HEW offices around the country, including sit-ins at the Washington HEW headquarters building and the San Francisco regional office. The protests received extensive media attention, and the San Francisco sit-in lasted for twenty-eight days, until the disputed Section 504 regulations were finally issued by Secretary Califano. The disability rights movement had won a visible national victory that led to major improvements in public access and official recognition of the legitimacy of their objectives.

This accomplishment generated great momentum for the movement for disability rights. New activist groups were formed around the country, including one focusing on access to public transportation in Denver, Colorado. This group, American Disabled for Accessible Public Transit (ADAPT), was founded by wheelchair users from a Denver independent living center in 1978 and led by Wade Blank, a nondisabled minister and health activist. ADAPT's founders engaged in public protests by crawling up the stairs of inaccessible buses and using the slogan "We Will Ride!"

Another important manifestation of the disability rights movement was a series of Deaf President Now protests at Gallaudet University in 1988. Gallaudet is a federally chartered university in Washington, D.C., whose primary mission is to serve deaf and hearing impaired students. Gallaudet had always been governed by senior administrators who were not deaf and were not recruited from the culturally Deaf community. When the university presidency became vacant and a hearing person was named to replace him, activist students erupted in six days of protests, protests that were encouraged by Deaf activists in the broader community of Gallaudet alumni. The students were successful in attaining the resignation of the hearing candidate, Elizabeth Zinser, and in the subsequent appointment of I. King Jordan, a deaf Gallaudet administrator, as university president.

The Americans with Disabilities Act Becomes Law

For many disability rights activists, the culmination of their struggle was the enactment of the Americans with Disabilities Act [ADA] in 1990. This law went far beyond Section 504 in guaranteeing rights of access and nondiscrimination in private employment, public accommodations, state and local governmental programs and facilities, and telecommunications. The ADA was first proposed by the National Council on Disability (NCD), a presidentially appointed advisory board, in 1987. While the members of NCD at that time had been appointed by the conservative President Ronald Reagan, they included several strong disability rights advocates with ties to the Republican

Party, such as Justin Dart. NCD and its organizational allies in the disability community conducted a national campaign in the late 1980s to build support for the ADA and were finally successful in gaining its near-unanimous Congressional passage in 1990, after which it was signed into law by President George H.W. Bush.

The ADA states its purpose as follows:

(1) to provide a clear and comprehensive national mandate for the elimination of discrimination against individuals with disabilities; (2) to provide clear, strong, consistent, enforceable standards addressing discrimination against individuals with disabilities; (3) to ensure that the Federal Government plays a central role in enforcing the standards . . . on behalf of individuals with disabilities; and (4) to invoke the sweep of congressional authority, including the power to enforce the fourteenth amendment and to regulate commerce, in order to address the major areas of discrimination faced day-to-day by people with disabilities.

Disability rights activists had hoped that the ADA would lead to significant improvements for Americans with disabilities, not only by opening up new opportunities in the affected areas but by bringing about a major reassessment by the American public and in institutions across the society of the need to include Americans with disabilities in the American dream. Nearly two decades after the ADA's enactment, nearly all observers agree that this reassessment has not come about. Americans with disabilities continue to have lower incomes, to have lower educational attainment, to be disproportionately unemployed and underemployed, to reside in residential facilities against their will, and to be the subject of stigma and exclusion in many spheres of public life.

One explanation for this continuing situation is a series of judicial decisions that have narrowed the ADA's impact. Federal courts have ruled that Congress lacks the constitutional authority to overturn discriminatory actions by states against their citizens with disabilities, that many accommodations sought by disabled employees or customers of retail establishments are unreasonable and therefore need not be provided, that people with many less severe disabilities lack standing to claim protection under the ADA, and that people with more severe disabilities are not entitled to relief because of their conditions. In 2008, Congress passed the ADA Restoration Act, which President George W. Bush signed into law on September 25, 2008. Disability rights advocates are hopeful that this legislation will overturn some of these adverse rulings, but its actual impact will remain unclear and dependent on future judicial rulings and a commitment by the federal executive branch to vigorous legal enforcement.

Self-Advocacy Makes a Difference

The self-advocacy groups that comprise the current disability rights movement were established incrementally since the nineteenth century, but the movement reached a critical political mass in the 1970s, with a wide array of organizations engaged in political activities and achieving legislative and judicial victories. The very practice of organizing for social change has made a significant difference for Americans with disabilities, promoting a model for political action and civic engagement while helping to create both local and national communities, within and across types of impairment, in which disabled people play a central, self-determined role. The existence of self-advocacy organizations has thus been instrumental in the pursuit of rights for disabled people but has also promoted independent lives in which disability is a positive connection rather than simply a stigmatized status.

Beyond the empowerment of acting collectively on one's own behalf, however, concrete gains have been made by disability rights advocates. Millions of children have benefited from public education since the enactment of IDEA. Public and private buildings, transit vehicles, and telecommunication devices are far more accessible than before Section 504 was passed in 1974 and the ADA became law in 1990. And despite the persistence of stigma, stereotypes, and physical and procedural barriers, Americans with disabilities have become more integrated with the societal mainstream and more accepted in their differences than was true before the advent of a movement for disability rights.

> "[Public institutions] should dedicate themselves to providing physical conditions and treatment programs . . . that substantially exceed medical and constitutional minimums."

Mentally Disabled Individuals Must Receive Minimum Levels of Care Within Institutions

The Circuit Court's Decision

Frank Minis Johnson Jr.

Following the layoff of almost one hundred employees at Bryce Hospital, a public institution for the mentally disabled in Tuscaloosa, Alabama, two attorneys filed a class-action lawsuit, Wyatt v. Stickney, *against the Alabama Department of Mental Health and Stonewall Stickney, the department's commissioner. They contended that the layoffs would create a situation in which the involuntarily committed patients of the institution would not receive adequate treatment. After hearing the case, Judge Frank Minis Johnson Jr. ruled on March 21, 1971, that state institutions must provide a minimum level of care to their patients in accordance with the US Constitution. In the following viewpoint, which is Johnson's ruling, the judge provides a specific set of standards that must be followed by all state institutions in Alabama. The standards can be categorized under three main headings: humane psychological and*

Frank Minis Johnson Jr., *Wyatt v. Stickney*, US Supreme Court, April 13, 1972.

physical environments, sufficient staffing, and individualized treatment plans. These guidelines served as the basis for the operations of mental institutions until a judge ruled in 2003 that state institutions had succeeded in implementing a minimum standard of care. Frank Minis Johnson Jr. served as a federal judge in Alabama from 1955 until his death in 1999.

This class action originally was filed on October 23, 1970, in behalf of patients involuntarily confined for mental treatment purposes at Bryce Hospital, Tuscaloosa, Alabama. On March 12, 1971, in a formal opinion and decree, this Court held that these involuntarily committed patients "unquestionably have a constitutional right to receive such individual treatment as will give each of them a realistic opportunity to be cured or to improve his or her mental condition." The Court further held that patients at Bryce were being denied their right to treatment and that defendants, per their request, would be allowed six months in which to raise the level of care at Bryce to the constitutionally required minimum. . . .

On September 23, 1971, defendants filed their final report, from which this Court concluded on December 10, 1971, that defendants had failed to promulgate and implement a treatment program satisfying minimum medical and constitutional requisites. Generally, the Court found that defendants' treatment program was deficient in three fundamental areas. It failed to provide: (1) a humane psychological and physical environment, (2) qualified staff in numbers sufficient to administer adequate treatment and (3) individualized treatment plans. More specifically, the Court found that many conditions, such as nontherapeutic, uncompensated work assignments, and the absence of any semblance of privacy, constituted dehumanizing factors contributing to the degeneration of the patients' self-esteem. The physical facilities at Bryce were overcrowded and plagued by fire and other emergency hazards. The Court found also that most staff members were poorly trained and that staffing ratios were so inadequate as to render the administration of effective treatment impossible. The Court concluded, therefore, that whatever treatment was provided at Bryce was grossly deficient and failed to satisfy minimum medical and constitutional standards. . . .

Pursuant to this order, a hearing was held at which the foremost authorities on mental health in the United States appeared and testified as to the minimum medical and constitutional requisites for public institutions, such as Bryce and Searcy [Hospital in Mount Vernon, Alabama], designed to treat the mentally ill. At this hearing, the parties and amici [friends of the court] submitted their proposed standards, and now have filed briefs in support of them. Moreover, the parties and amici have stipulated to a broad spectrum of conditions they feel are mandatory for a constitutionally acceptable minimum treatment program. This Court, having considered the evidence in the case, as well as the briefs, proposed standards and stipulations of the parties, has concluded that the standards set out in Appendix A to this decree are medical and constitutional minimums. Consequently, the Court will order their implementation. In so ordering, however, the Court emphasizes that these standards are, indeed, both medical and constitutional minimums and should be viewed as such. The Court urges that once this order is effectuated, defendants not become complacent and self-satisfied. Rather, they should dedicate themselves to providing physical conditions and treatment programs at Alabama's mental institutions that substantially exceed medical and constitutional minimums. . . .

Patients Must Be Provided a Humane Psychological and Physical Environment

1. Patients have a right to privacy and dignity.
2. Patients have a right to the least restrictive conditions necessary to achieve the purposes of commitment.
3. No person shall be deemed incompetent to manage his

affairs, to contract, to hold professional or occupational or vehicle operator's licenses, to marry and obtain a divorce, to register and vote, or to make a will *solely* by reason of his admission or commitment to the hospital.

4. Patients shall have the same rights to visitation and telephone communications as patients at other public hospitals, except to the extent that the Qualified Mental Health Professional responsible for formulation of a particular patient's treatment plan writes an order imposing special restrictions. The written order must be renewed after each periodic review of the treatment plan if any restrictions are to be continued. Patients shall have an unrestricted right to visitation with attorneys and with private physicians and other health professionals.

5. Patients shall have an unrestricted right to send sealed mail. Patients shall have an unrestricted right to receive sealed mail from their attorneys, private physicians, and other mental health professionals, from courts, and government officials. Patients shall have a right to receive sealed mail from others, except to the extent that the Qualified Mental Health Professional responsible for formulation of a particular patient's treatment plan writes an order imposing special restrictions on receipt of sealed mail. The written order must be renewed after each periodic review of the treatment plan if any restrictions are to be continued.

6. Patients have a right to be free from unnecessary or excessive medication. No medication shall be administered unless at the written order of a physician. The superintendent of the hospital and the attending physician shall be responsible for all medication given or administered to a patient. The use of medication shall not exceed standards of use that are advocated by the United States Food and Drug Administration. Notation of each individual's medication shall be kept in his medical records. At least weekly the at-

tending physician shall review the drug regimen of each patient under his care. All prescriptions shall be written with a termination date, which shall not exceed 30 days. Medication shall not be used as punishment, for the convenience of staff, as a substitute for program, or in quantities that interfere with the patient's treatment program.

7. Patients have a right to be free from physical restraint and isolation. Except for emergency situations, in which it is likely that patients could harm themselves or others and in which less restrictive means of restraint are not feasible, patients may be physically restrained or placed in isolation only on a Qualified Mental Health Professional's written order which explains the rationale for such action. The written order may be entered only after the Qualified Mental Health Professional has personally seen the patient concerned and evaluated whatever episode or situation is said to call for restraint or isolation. Emergency use of restraints or isolation shall be for no more than one hour, by which time a Qualified Mental Health Professional shall have been consulted and shall have entered an appropriate order in writing. Such written order shall be effective for no more than 24 hours and must be renewed if restraint and isolation are to be continued. While in restraint or isolation the patient must be seen by qualified ward personnel who will chart the patient's physical condition (if it is compromised) and psychiatric condition every hour. The patient must have bathroom privileges every hour and must be bathed every 12 hours.

8. Patients shall have a right not to be subjected to experimental research without the express and informed consent of the patient, if the patient is able to give such consent, and of his guardian or next of kin, after opportunities for consultation with independent specialists and with legal counsel. Such proposed research shall first have been reviewed and approved by the institution's Human Rights Committee

before such consent shall be sought. Prior to such approval the Committee shall determine that such research complies with the principles of the Statement on the Use of Human Subjects for Research of the American Association on Mental Deficiency and with the principles for research involving human subjects required by the United States Department of Health, Education and Welfare for projects supported by that agency.

9. Patients have a right not to be subjected to treatment procedures such as lobotomy, electro-convulsive treatment, adversive reinforcement conditioning or other unusual or hazardous treatment procedures without their express and informed consent after consultation with counsel or interested party of the patient's choice.

10. Patients have a right to receive prompt and adequate medical treatment for any physical ailments.

11. Patients have a right to wear their own clothes and to keep and use their own personal possessions except insofar as such clothes or personal possessions may be determined by a Qualified Mental Health Professional to be dangerous or otherwise inappropriate to the treatment regimen.

12. The hospital has an obligation to supply an adequate allowance of clothing to any patients who do not have suitable clothing of their own. Patients shall have the opportunity to select from various types of neat, clean, and seasonable clothing. Such clothing shall be considered the patient's throughout his stay in the hospital.

13. The hospital shall make provision for the laundering of patient clothing.

14. Patients have a right to regular physical exercise several times a week. Moreover, it shall be the duty of the hospital to provide facilities and equipment for such exercise.

15. Patients have a right to be outdoors at regular and frequent intervals, in the absence of medical considerations.

Wyatt v. Stickney Revolutionized Patient Care and Rights

Wyatt's domestic impact outside of Alabama was significant . . . there being "no doubt" of its "massive influence" on the development of state-level Patients' Bills of Rights; the promulgation of rights-enforcing regulations in nearly three-quarters of all states; and a host of federal legislation including Section 504 of the Rehabilitation Act of 1973, the Mental Health Systems Act [1980], the Protection and Advocacy for Individuals with Mental Illness Act (PAIMI Act) [1998], and the Developmental Disabilities Assistance and Bill of Rights Act [2000]. The state laws inspired by *Wyatt* "established baseline civil rights governing the substantive and procedural limitations on the involuntary civil commitment process, the right to treatment, and the right to refuse treatment." Beyond that, the *Wyatt* mandate of a right to treatment in the least restrictive alternative is "echoed in the Americans with Disabilities Act," as articulated in *Olmstead v. L.C.* [1999]. There is no dispute that *Wyatt* was "the beginning of a revolution" recognizing the rights of institutionalized persons with mental disabilities.

Michael L. Perlin, "'Abandoned Love': The Impact of Wyatt v. Stickney *on the Intersection Between International Human Rights and Domestic Mental Disability Law,*" Law & Psychology Review, *January 1, 2011.*

16. The right to religious worship shall be accorded to each patient who desires such opportunities. Provisions for such worship shall be made available to all patients on a non-discriminatory basis. No individual shall be coerced into engaging in any religious activities.

17. The institution shall provide, with adequate supervision, suitable opportunities for the patient's interaction with members of the opposite sex. . . .

Patient Labor Must Be Voluntary

No patient shall be required to perform labor which involves the operation and maintenance of the hospital or for which the hospital is under contract with an outside organization. Privileges or release from the hospital shall not be conditioned upon the performance of labor covered by this provision. Patients may voluntarily engage in such labor if the labor is compensated in accordance with the minimum wage laws of the Fair Labor Standards Act, 1966.

(1) Patients may be required to perform therapeutic tasks which do not involve the operation and maintenance of the hospital, provided the specific task or any change in assignment is:

    a. An integrated part of the patient's treatment plan and approved as a therapeutic activity by a Qualified Mental Health Professional responsible for supervising the patient's treatment; and

    b. Supervised by a staff member to oversee the therapeutic aspects of the activity.

(2) Patients may voluntarily engage in therapeutic labor for which the hospital would otherwise have to pay an employee, provided the specific labor or any change in labor assignment is:

    a. An integrated part of the patient's treatment plan and approved as a therapeutic activity by a Qualified Mental Health Professional responsible for supervising the patient's treatment; and

    b. Supervised by a staff member to oversee the therapeutic aspects of the activity; and

    c. Compensated in accordance with the minimum wage laws of the Fair Labor Standards Act, 1966.

Patients may be required to perform tasks of a personal housekeeping nature such as the making of one's own bed.

Payment to patients pursuant to these paragraphs shall not be applied to the costs of hospitalization.

Institution Facilities Should Provide the Optimum Opportunity for Treatment

A patient has a right to a humane psychological and physical environment within the hospital facilities. These facilities shall be designed to afford patients with comfort and safety, promote dignity, and ensure privacy. The facilities shall be designed to make a positive contribution to the efficient attainment of the treatment goals of the hospital.

The number of patients in a multi-patient room shall not exceed six persons. There shall be allocated a minimum of 80 square feet of floor space per patient in a multi-patient room. Screens or curtains shall be provided to ensure privacy within the resident unit. Single rooms shall have a minimum of 100 square feet of floor space. Each patient will be furnished with a comfortable bed with adequate changes of linen, a closet or locker for his personal belongings, a chair, and a bedside table.

There will be one toilet provided for each eight patients and one lavatory [sink with running water] for each six patients. A lavatory will be provided with each toilet facility. The toilets will be installed in separate stalls to ensure privacy, will be clean and free of odor, and will be equipped with appropriate safety devices for the physically handicapped.

There will be one tub or shower for each 15 patients. If a central bathing area is provided, each shower area will be divided by curtains to ensure privacy. Showers and tubs will be equipped with adequate safety accessories.

The minimum day room area shall be 40 square feet per patient. Day rooms will be attractive and adequately furnished with reading lamps, tables, chairs, television and other recreational facilities. They will be conveniently located to patients' bedrooms and shall have outside windows. There shall be at least one day room area on each bedroom floor in a multi-story hospital. Areas used for corridor traffic cannot be counted as day room space; nor can a chapel with fixed pews be counted as a day room area.

The historic Bryce Hospital in Tuscaloosa, Alabama, played a major role in disability rights laws in the United States. Following the firing of one hundred employees at Bryce Hospital, Wyatt v. Stickney (1971) ruled that state institutions must provide a minimum level of care to their patients. © Jay Reeves/AP Images.

The minimum dining room area shall be ten square feet per patient. The dining room shall be separate from the kitchen and will be furnished with comfortable chairs and tables with hard, washable surfaces.

The hospital shall provide adequate facilities and equipment for handling clean and soiled bedding and other linen. There must be frequent changes of bedding and other linen, no less than every seven days to assure patient comfort.

Regular housekeeping and maintenance procedures which will ensure that the hospital is maintained in a safe, clean, and attractive condition will be developed and implemented.

There must be special facilities for geriatric and other non-ambulatory patients to assure their safety and comfort, including special fittings on toilets and wheelchairs. Appropriate provision shall be made to permit nonambulatory patients to communicate their needs to staff. . . .

Sufficient Numbers of Qualified Staff Must Be Employed

Each Qualified Mental Health Professional shall meet all licensing and certification requirements promulgated by the State of Alabama for persons engaged in private practice of the same profession elsewhere in Alabama. Other staff members shall meet the same licensing and certification requirements as persons who engage in private practice of their specialty elsewhere in Alabama.

    a. All Non-Professional Staff Members who have not had prior clinical experience in a mental institution shall have a substantial orientation training.

    b. Staff members on all levels shall have regularly scheduled in-service training.

Each Non-Professional Staff Member shall be under the direct supervision of a Qualified Mental Health Professional.

The hospital shall have the following minimum numbers of treatment personnel per 250 patients. Qualified Mental Health Professionals trained in particular disciplines may in appropriate situations perform services or functions traditionally performed by members of other disciplines. Changes in staff deployment may be made with prior approval of this Court upon a clear and convincing demonstration that the proposed deviation from this staffing structure will enhance the treatment of the patients. . . .

Each Patient Will Receive an Individualized Treatment Plan

Each patient shall have a comprehensive physical and mental examination and review of behavioral status within 48 hours after admission to the hospital.

Each patient shall have an individualized treatment plan. This plan shall be developed by appropriate Qualified Mental Health Professionals, including a psychiatrist, and implemented as soon as possible—in any event no later than five days after the patient's admission. . . .

As part of his treatment plan, each patient shall have an individualized post-hospitalization plan. This plan shall be developed by a Qualified Mental Health Professional as soon as practicable after the patient's admission to the hospital. . . .

Complete patient records shall be kept on the ward in which the patient is placed and shall be available to anyone properly authorized in writing by the patient. . . .

In addition to complying with all the other standards herein, a hospital shall make special provisions for the treatment of patients who are children and young adults. . . .

No later than 15 days after a patient is committed to the hospital, the superintendent of the hospital or his appointed, professionally qualified agent shall examine the committed patient and shall determine whether the patient continues to require hospitalization and whether a treatment plan . . . has been implemented. If the patient no longer requires hospitalization in accordance with the standards for commitment, or if a treatment plan has not been implemented, he must be released immediately unless he agrees to continue with treatment on a voluntary basis.

> *"The courts . . . have in large measure conceptualized the problems of institutions in simplistic terms . . . of over-crowding, understaffing, and underfinancing."*

Mandating Minimum Levels of Care Could Impede Care in Institutions

Charles C. Cleland and Gary V. Sluyter

Following the 1971 ruling in Wyatt v. Stickney, *which mandated a minimum standard of care in Alabama state institutions, some skepticism existed about the perceived positive impact of the decision. In the following viewpoint, Charles C. Cleland and Gary V. Sluyter, two individuals associated with the Texas Department of Mental Health and Mental Retardation at the time, contend that the state-imposed minimum standards of care had the potential to damage instead of improve the mental health system. They object to the guideline that mandates an increase in the number of employees at the hospitals and argue that this increase in staffing could result in staff discontent, which could lead to decreased care and a strain on the physical landscape of the institutions. Further, they point out that the funding to meet these guidelines would have to come from a reallocation of money away from newly favored,*

Charles C. Cleland and Gary V. Sluyter, "The Alabama Decision: Unequivocal Blessing," *Community Mental Health Journal,* vol. 10, no. 4, 1974, pp. 409–510. Copyright © 1974 by Springer. All rights reserved. Reproduced by permission.

community-based modes of treatment, thus hindering the posi-
tive momentum of these programs. They conclude that the ruling's
mandates are too simplistic to provide meaningful reform.

It is becoming a painfully conscious fact that institutions for the mentally retarded and mentally ill are under attack in this country (Shafter, 1971). That this offensive is beginning to carry judicial authority has been amply demonstrated in various right-to-treatment court battles, notably those in Alabama, New York, Georgia, and Massachusetts. Most of these remain in some stage of litigation as of this writing [1974], but one that promises to have some of the most far-reaching implications for the future appears to be the Alabama decision (*Wyatt vs Stickney, Civil Action No. 3195-N, M.D. Alabama*). In that case, to assume adequate treatment by a public institution, the U.S. District Court, ". . . has laid down 49 objectively measurable and judicially enforceable guidelines with which it has required the State to comply. [Freedman, 1972]." These guidelines included minimum standards for treatment, staffing patterns, and a detailed procedure for their implication.

The fact that the courts have seen fit to intervene in the administration of public facilities for the retarded and mentally ill is disturbing enough for those charged with this responsibility. Even more disturbing, perhaps, is the fact that the courts, advised by a series of *amici curiae*, have in large measure conceptualized the problems of institutions in simplistic terms and have focused their charges Quixote fashion on the menacing triple windmill of over-crowding, understaffing, and underfinancing (Kugel, 1969). By suggesting the time-worn solutions of more money, larger staffs, and less residents, the courts have fallen into the trap of producing those "simpleminded, low-level measures" which [Wolf] Wolfensberger (1969) warned could not adequately replace a lack of models and concepts.

It is the intention of this paper to examine the implications of the Alabama decision in light of current administrative theory and research as well as current trends in the delivery of services to the mentally ill or retarded. By so doing, more substantive solutions may occur to administrative and program-oriented institutional employees.

In this respect it appears that in the Alabama decision the courts have overlooked several critical implications of the actions so adjudicated—that is, budget considerations, cost-personnel factors, effects of growth, and the rate of growth.

Budget Conflict

The timing of the Alabama decision in relation to broader-scale occurrences within the field of mental retardation or mental illness seems ironic, at best. The demand for community-based services as alternatives to institutional care has been growing steadily over the past decade. Even institutions themselves have joined this movement by contributing some of their own resources to programs such as outreach or community services (Sluyter, 1969). Serious consideration of the Alabama staffing patterns would appear to have the potential for rechanneling already scarce funds away from the community and back into the residential facility for its internal operations.

One example of this unsteady balance between resources for community-based versus institutional-based programs is emerging at this writing on the federal level. A bill now under consideration in Congress would authorize funds to aid state institutions in meeting Joint Accreditations Commission (Chicago, 1971) standards for residential facilities. . . . The question rises as to the overall effects of competing funds on such struggling new community-oriented programs as the developmental disabilities legislation. It seems logical to assume that already underfunded programs such as this would be cut back even further if Congress were to commit additional large sums to institutions. And it seems unlikely that at a time of many competing demands for domestic spending one can have his cake and eat it as well.

Cost Personnel Factors

The effects of the Alabama decision on available funds for other types of programs is one thing, the practical implications for institutional budgets is another. The projected budgetary increase for staff alone at Partlow State School in Alabama is unknown to these authors, but in another state it has been estimated that to comply with the staffing patterns as outlined would double the present institutional budgets. In addition, almost 10,000 new employees would need to be hired for the entire state system. Among these would be 26 physicians, 161 psychologists, 961 special education teachers, and 7,235 attendants. Even if the state legislature were to provide sufficient funds, the problem of finding and recruiting sufficient and adequately trained personnel appears insurmountable. To hire enough physicians alone (in a state with only one available for every 830 population) would be almost impossible.

Regarding staffing patterns, the courts have not only gone far beyond the letter and spirit of the new Joint Commission standards, they have jumped off into an area almost completely lacking in empirical support, as will be shown.

Effects of Growth

The presumed or hypothetical benefits that may derive from enormous staff increments of institutions are somewhat easier to envision than the reverse. In part, the reason is historical. For decades institutions coped, albeit poorly, with an abysmally small employee work force. One Texas facility just 20 years ago had 2,100 residents and 395 employees to cover three shifts. Today the same facility has about 1,850 residents, 1,200 authorized employees, and many volunteers. Obviously, "soldiering" on the job with so few fellow workers was easily spotted by the superintendent and more harshly dealt with by *working* employees. Worker productivity is not, nor are increased staff-resident interactions, a foregone conclusion. Only the most naive person would harbor such expectations. [Peter] Kong-Ming and [Josephine] Callahan (1959) studied the effects of greatly increasing the number of nurses in a

Wyatt v. Stickney *(1971) established minimum standards of care for state-run mental institutions. Some maintain that the staffing increase mandate imposed by* Wyatt *will hinder the mental health system by causing staff discontent and a decreased level of care.* © Laflor/ E+/Getty Images.

general hospital and found that "patient-nursing hours changed very little." Again, in a similar vein Drucker (1964) has pointed out that overstaffing is a prime time waster and when "senior people in the group spend more than about one-tenth of their time on problems of 'human relations,' then the work force is almost certainly too large." Another potential outcome of overstaffing, one that industrial managers have observed, is boredom. In a recent training session with institutional supervisory employees, one of the authors received the comment, "I don't have enough to do. The work has gotten boring, can you tell me how to make it interesting again?"

What other considerations do large increments in the work force call to our attention? Workers, unlike the residents, can bring interesting space requirements to bear on the institution. If a thousand employees are added, and one-third bring cars into the facility—that is, 333 autos—each requiring approximately 300 square feet per car (Muther, 1970), we have eroded a total of

99,900 square feet or over 2 acres of space; this is space that may have been in trees, shrubbery (excellent noise baffles), or play space for the residents. These burgeoning asphalt jungles have been discussed in [an article by Charles C.] Cleland and [Jon D.] Swartz (1972) and need no further mention here. They do impair the ecological aspects of institutions unless carefully considered. Thinking further along an ecological line we see there is more to muddy the waters! With a possible doubling of the existing institutional work force, noise levels will be magnified considerably. In many sectors of the institution this will complicate both communications and safety. [V.A.] Graicunas (Terry, 1956) advanced the theory that as additional persons are added to an organization, the relationships do not increase in the same proportion as the persons added, but at a much greater rate. He then demonstrated that when a fourth subordinate is added, the total relationships jump from 18 to 44, an increase of over 140%. Most parents know this intuitively; that is, when the number of children increases, communications become more and more complex. Many other interesting and often unforeseeable consequences attend what is so obviously a plus—that is, more staff—and some of these are discussed in Cleland (1965).

Rate of Growth

How can a large number of new employees be assimilated into an institution? This problem can be more clearly conceptualized by thinking at the level of a family. Humans usually reproduce singly but suppose we consider a family of five—mother, father, and three children. Pregnancy occurs again and this time, triplets. We have here an illustration of doubling the number of children, resulting in an enormously more complex family organization that demands a near abandonment of the previous needs of the existing family members. However, quintuplets (a very rare occurrence) would actually double the total family size and this is somewhat analogous to what is envisioned for the large-scale organization termed "institution." Although

The Least Restrictive Environment Standard Is Flawed

When [professor of disability studies] Steve Taylor wrote [the article] *Caught in the Continuum* in 1988, he described the flawed thinking associated with the "least restrictive environment" (LRE) principle and the related continuum model of human services that linked severity of disability with segregation, and required improvements in skills as a prerequisite for moving from congregation to integration. . . . Furthermore, he argued that the flawed thinking that established educational, residential, and employment continuums carried over into community-based services. Steve Taylor prophesied that once you accept "continuum thinking," schools and communities cannot be fully inclusive. . . .

Taylor wrote that seven serious conceptual and philosophical flaws characterized the principle of LRE. The LRE principle: (1) legitimates restrictive environments, (2) confuses segregation and integration on the one hand with intensity of services on the other, (3) is based on a "readiness" model, (4) supports the primacy of professional decision making, (5) sanctions infringements on people's rights, (6) implies that people must move as they develop and change, and (7) directs attention to physical settings rather than to the services and supports people need to be integrated into the community.

Jan Nisbet, "'Caught in the Continuum,'"
Research and Practice for Persons with Severe
Disabilities *(RPSD), Winter 2004.*

this hypothetical family doubling occurs at an instant and the institutional employee growth rate (if the Alabama decision is followed elsewhere) will occur in 6 months time, there is one enormous difference. Employees will be adults and not under the constraints or direction parents exercise over children: They may join unions (Cleland and Brandt, 1970) and have a wide variety of values and attitudes that may be at considerable variance from those of the institutional authority or the prevailing philosophy. Thus by doubling the size of staff in so short a time, enormous opportunities for value clashes between the existent work force and the neophytes are created. An example of this, at the resident level, is easy to provide. At one point in the history of one of the nation's older institutions, some 400 residents (largely behavior-problem types) were transferred from several sister institutions into this unfortunate "dumping" institution. The institution at the time of the transfer had a population of about 800. The results were greatly increased numbers of fights, assaults, elopements, and even a murder. For employees, morale sagged and for 20 years subsequent to this dramatic occurrence, no superintendent lasted over 16 months. Interrogation of long-tenure employees about why this particular facility had such an enormous turnover at every level indicated that the blame could be squarely put on transferring into the institution, in a single week, half again the number of residents. As one staff member said, "It literally tore us up and no superintendent seemed able to right the ship." This example serves to underscore not only how quantity influences organizational behavior but also quality—in this case, loading the dice with other institutions' rejects. However, if one is unconvinced of the enormously complex task that appears ahead for institutions, attention should be directed toward certain aspects of literature on ethology, especially animal behavior. Crowding and litter size (grossly analogous to overstaffing) have led to cannibalism, highly abnormal sexual behavior, and various other behavioral aberrations (Galle, Gove, and McPherson, 1972), which for the species studied could hardly qualify as the animal equivalent of "normalization" (Nirje, 1969).

Only a decade ago the clamor was raised to limit the size of institutions; some recommendations were for no more than 250 residents, others were for up to 1,500 (Cleland, 1965). It seems both ironic and somewhat illogical to believe that only residents contribute to overcrowding. The current Alabama decision that would double staff size, in a sense, is implying employees cannot contribute to crowding or are insensitive to the same forces that act on retardates [mentally retarded persons]. Normalization cannot be applied to just one set of institutional actors—employees and retardates must be mutually addressed by such a concept. In conclusion, we do not know how much is too much. We do know, however, that size, staffing ratios, and so forth, are enormously more complex than the Alabama decision simplistically infers.

References

1. Cleland, C.C. Evidence on the relationship between size and institutional effectiveness: A review and analysis. *American Journal of Mental Deficiency*, 1965, 70, 423–431.
2. Cleland, C.C., & Swartz, J.D. *Administrative issues in institutions for the mentally retarded: Prescriptive practices and emergent issues.* Austin, Texas: Hogg Foundation for Mental Health, 1972.
3. Cleland, C.C., & Brandt, F.H. Unionzation of institutions: A therapeutic event. *Community Mental Health Journal*, 1970, 6, 51–62.
4. Drucker, P.F. *The concept of the organization.* New York: New American Library, 1964.
5. Freedman, P. *Mental retardation and the law.* Washington, D.C.: Office of Mental Retardation Coordination, 1972.
6. Galle, O.R., Gove, W.R., & McPherson, J.M. Population density and pathology: What are the relations for man? *Science*, 1972, 176, 23–30.
7. Kong-ming, N., & Callahan, J. *Nursing service and patient care: A staff experiment.* Kansas City: Community Studies, 1959.
8. Kugel, R.B. Why innovative action? In R.B. Kugel, & W. Wolfensberger (Eds.), *Changing patterns in residential services for the mentally retarded.* Washington, D.C.: President's Committee on Mental Retardation, 1969.
9. Muther, R. Plant layout and design. In H.B. Maynard (Ed.), *Handbook of business administration.* New York: McGraw-Hill, 1970.
10. Nirje, B. The normalization principle and its human management implications. In R.B. Kugel & W. Wolfensberger (Eds.), *Changing patterns in residential services for the mentally retarded.* Washington, D.C.: President's Commission on Mental Retardation, 1969.
11. Shafter, A.J. A philosophy of administration: A revisit. *Mental Retardation*, 1971, 9, 3–5.
12. Sluyter, G.V. The emergent role of the residential facility in the treatment and care of the community retardate. *Mental Retardation*, 1969, 7, 45–48.
13. Terry, G.R. *Principles of management.* Homewood, Ill.: Irwin, 1956.
14. Wolfensberger, W. The origin and nature of our institutional models. In R.B. Kugel, & W. Wolfensberger (Eds.), *Changing patterns in residential services for the mentally retarded.* Washington, D.C.: President's Committee on Mental Retardation, 1969.

> "A finding of 'mental illness' alone
> cannot justify a State's locking a
> person up against his will and keeping
> him indefinitely in simple custodial
> confinement."

States Cannot Hold Individuals in an Institution if They Do Not Present a Threat to Themselves or Others

The Supreme Court's Decision

Potter Stewart

While visiting his parents in Florida, Kenneth Donaldson told them that he suspected a neighbor of poisoning his food. Believing that his son was suffering from paranoid delusions, Donaldson's father had him committed to the Florida State mental health system in January 1957. Donaldson fought his confinement by filing a lawsuit, arguing that he was not mentally ill. After a district court found in Donaldson's favor in O'Connor v. Donaldson *[1975], awarding monetary damages and ordering his release, a series of appeals followed before the US Supreme Court affirmed the lower court's ruling in a unanimous decision. The following viewpoint presents this ruling, in which Justice Potter Stewart maintains that it is uncon-*

Potter Stewart, Opinion of the Court, *O'Connor v. Donaldson*, US Supreme Court, June 26, 1975.

stitutional to confine a person to an institution because he has been deemed mentally ill, if he does not present a threat to himself or others. Stewart equates this type of institutionalization with removing people from society whom the majority considers unfit to live among others based only on their appearance or difference from the norm. Appointed by President Dwight D. Eisenhower, Potter Stewart served as an associate justice of the Supreme Court from October 1958 until July 1981. He was known as a centrist who contributed to criminal justice reform, civil rights, court access, and interpretation of the Fourth Amendment.

The respondent, Kenneth Donaldson, was civilly committed to confinement as a mental patient in the Florida State Hospital at Chattahoochee in January 1957. He was kept in custody there against his will for nearly 15 years. The petitioner, Dr. J.B. O'Connor, was the hospital's superintendent during most of this period. Throughout his confinement Donaldson repeatedly, but unsuccessfully, demanded his release, claiming that he was dangerous to no one, that he was not mentally ill, and that, at any rate, the hospital was not providing treatment for his supposed illness. Finally, in February 1971, Donaldson brought this lawsuit under [statute] 42 U.S.C. 1983, in the United States District Court for the Northern District of Florida, alleging that O'Connor, and other members of the hospital staff named as defendants, had intentionally and maliciously deprived him of his constitutional right to liberty. . . .

Determining Everyone's Right to Constitutional Liberty

We have concluded that the difficult issues of constitutional law dealt with by the Court of Appeals are not presented by this case in its present posture. Specifically, there is no reason now to decide whether mentally ill persons dangerous to themselves or to others have a right to treatment upon compulsory confinement by the State, or whether the State may compulsorily confine a

US Supreme Court Justice Potter Stewart's decision in O'Connor v. Donaldson *(1975) ruled that the state cannot incarcerate an individual based on mental illness alone.* © Rob Dobi/ Flickr Open/Getty Images.

nondangerous, mentally ill individual for the purpose of treatment. As we view it, this case raises a single, relatively simple, but nonetheless important question concerning every man's constitutional right to liberty.

The jury found that Donaldson was neither dangerous to himself nor dangerous to others, and also found that, if mentally ill, Donaldson had not received treatment. That verdict, based on abundant evidence, makes the issue before the Court a narrow one. We need not decide whether, when, or by what procedures, a mentally ill person may be confined by the State on any of the grounds which, under contemporary statutes, are generally advanced to justify involuntary confinement of such a person—to prevent injury to the public, to ensure his own survival or safety, or to alleviate or cure his illness. For the jury found that none of the above grounds for continued confinement was present in Donaldson's case.

Given the jury's findings, what was left as justification for keeping Donaldson in continued confinement? The fact that state law may have authorized confinement of the harmless mentally ill does not itself establish a constitutionally adequate purpose for the confinement. Nor is it enough that Donaldson's original confinement was founded upon a constitutionally adequate basis, if in fact it was, because even if his involuntary confinement was initially permissible, it could not constitutionally continue after that basis no longer existed.

Mental Illness Alone Does Not Justify Confinement

A finding of "mental illness" alone cannot justify a State's locking a person up against his will and keeping him indefinitely in simple custodial confinement. Assuming that that term can be given a reasonably precise content and that the "mentally ill" can be identified with reasonable accuracy, there is still no constitutional basis for confining such persons involuntarily if they are dangerous to no one and can live safely in freedom.

O'Connor v. Donaldson Left Many Questions Unanswered

If the *Donaldson* decision has not hurt the right to treatment movement, it has certainly left a number of questions unanswered. Does
a civilly committed dangerous person have a right to release? If
treatment is provided, can commitment be prolonged? If treatment
is provided but is not effective, is there justification for continued
confinement of nondangerous persons? If a mentally ill person
could survive safely in freedom with some assistance, does society
have an obligation to provide help by increasing the numbers of
community based residential and treatment programs? It has been
postulated that the Supreme Court's narrow decision in *O'Connor v.
Donaldson* demonstrated its reluctance to consider these issues.

*Lester B. Brown and Jeanne M. Bremer, "In-
adequate Means to a Noble End: The Right to
Treatment Paradox,"* Journal of Psychiatry and
Law, *Spring 1978.*

May the State confine the mentally ill merely to ensure them
a living standard superior to that they enjoy in the private community? That the State has a proper interest in providing care and
assistance to the unfortunate goes without saying. But the mere
presence of mental illness does not disqualify a person from
preferring his home to the comforts of an institution. Moreover,
while the State may arguably confine a person to save him from
harm, incarceration is rarely if ever a necessary condition for
raising the living standards of those capable of surviving safely
in freedom, on their own or with the help of family or friends.

May the State fence in the harmless mentally ill solely to save
its citizens from exposure to those whose ways are different? One
might as well ask if the State, to avoid public unease, could incarcerate all who are physically unattractive or socially eccentric.

Mere public intolerance or animosity cannot constitutionally justify the deprivation of a person's physical liberty.

In short, a State cannot constitutionally confine without more a nondangerous individual who is capable of surviving safely in freedom by himself or with the help of willing and responsible family members or friends. Since the jury found, upon ample evidence, that O'Connor, as an agent of the State, knowingly did so confine Donaldson, it properly concluded that O'Connor violated Donaldson's constitutional right to freedom.

> *"The Supreme Court did not provide standards for 'adequate treatment' or for separating the nondangerous from the dangerous patient."*

The Court's Ruling on Institutionalization of the Mentally Disabled Lacks Strength

J.L. Bernard

Following the ruling in the 1975 US Supreme Court case O'Connor v. Donaldson, *many hailed the decision as establishing the right to treatment within state-run, mental-health institutions. While J.L. Bernard admits this significance in the following viewpoint, he argues that the court's failing to concretely define the terms "dangerous" and "treatment" creates a situation in which lower courts are left to interpret the ruling, thus diminishing its influence. Bernard contends that because the ruling deals only with the issues directly addressed in the case, namely whether a nondangerous individual can be confined without the provision of adequate treatment, lower courts are left to determine whether an individual is dangerous based on the analysis of psychiatrists who have been shown in the past to be wrong in their assessments.*

J.L. Bernard, "The Significance for Psychology of O'Connor v. Donaldson," *American Psychologist*, vol. 32, no. 12, December 1977, pp. 1085–1088. Copyright © 1977 by American Psychological Association. Reproduced with permission.

*Further, without a concrete basis establishing what adequate treat-
ment entails, lower courts similarly must leave all the decisions
about treatment to outside parties. Bernard believes that psychology can play an important role in filling the gaps left by this ruling.
J.L. Bernard was an attorney and clinical psychology professor at
Memphis State University.*

Recently [in 1975], the Supreme Court of the United States,
in *O'Connor v. Donaldson*, handed down a decision with the
potential for as much impact on the institutionalized mentally ill
as *Brown v. Board of Education* [1954] had for eliminating de-
segregation in the public schools. In *O'Connor v. Donaldson*, for
the first time, the Supreme Court recognized a constitutional basis for a "right to treatment" for the nondangerous mentally ill
and in essence said that the state could not confine them against
their wills unless such treatment was provided. As with *Brown*,
in which the Court stated the law but left its implementation to
the lower courts (a task still incomplete after two decades), the
holding in *O'Connor* will be controlling on lower courts in future
litigation by patients claiming they are not receiving adequate
treatment. But these courts are in very serious need of expert assistance from the behavioral sciences if their rulings are to be just.

Due Process Must Be Followed in State Confinement Hearings

A typical state commitment statute justifies the involuntary confinement of the mentally ill on two grounds: (a) The mentally ill
are dangerous to themselves or others, and (b) they are in need
of care and treatment. Any psychologist who has served on the
staff of a typical state mental institution is aware that, for the majority of patients, the "care and treatment" provided amounts to
what the court in *Nason v. Superintendent of Bridgewater State
Hospital* characterized as "three meals a day and a bed." What
the Supreme Court has held in *O'Connor* amounts to saying that
treatment is a *quid pro quo* [something given or received for

Psychiatrists' Values Trump Civil Rights

After the Supreme Court decision in *O'Connor v. Donaldson*, and federal district court cases such as *Lessard v. Schmidt*, imposed substantial substantive and procedural protections on states' civil commitment processes, much promise existed that psychiatrists would be prohibited from imposing their values as to what is best for someone at the expense of civil liberties. It did not happen. Like the defeated confederacy after the Civil War, much of institutional psychiatry made clear its disdain for the new legal order and challenged those in a position to enforce the newly established legal norms to force change. With a few exceptions, little has happened. Again, with exceptions, lawyers for civilly committed patients have ceded their adversary role and tiptoed gingerly in the courtroom. To a significant degree, courts have abandoned their role of neutral arbiters. In addition, the amorphous concept of danger, a constitutional standard that was supposed to significantly limit commitments, has significantly contributed to psychiatrists continuing to impose their values in an unchecked manner. It is time for lawyers and courts to step up.

> William M. Brooks, "The Tail Still Wags the Dog: The Pervasive and Inappropriate Influence by the Psychiatric Profession on the Civil Commitment Process," North Dakota Law Review, January 1, 2010.

something else] for confinement. Within this context it should be borne in mind that the 14th Amendment to the Constitution prohibits the states from depriving an individual of life, liberty, or property without "due process of law." This signifies that before anyone may be confined against his or her will, be it in a prison or hospital, two criteria of fairness must be met: (a) Procedures ensuring a fair hearing (notice of the hearing, the right to be present at the hearing and to be represented by counsel, etc.) must be followed, and (b) the law justifying the commitment must be fair and just. Should it be assumed that the mentally ill have always enjoyed these fundamental protections of individual liberty (as must any criminal), it should be noted that during 1974, commitment statutes in Alabama (*Lynch v. Baxley*) and Michigan (*Bell v. Wayne County General Hospital at Eloise*) were overturned by federal courts for failing to provide these basic constitutional guarantees. That this is part of a continuing trend may be seen in *Suzuki v. Quisenberry* [1976], in which segments of Hawaii's commitment statute were struck down because they violated the 14th Amendment's due-process clause.

Establishing Treatment Guidelines

The concern of the legal profession with the rights of the involuntarily committed mental patient is of fairly recent development. [American attorney Morton] Birnbaum is generally credited with being "the father of the right to treatment" for having suggested to the legal fraternity that if an individual was to be deprived of his or her liberty because he or she "needed treatment," the state should be obliged to provide that treatment. It was 6 years later that a major federal court in *Rouse v. Cameron* [1966] held that this was a valid constitutional argument. In *Rouse*, Judge David Bazelon, an outspoken advocate of just treatment for the mentally ill, invited the medical professional to work in tandem with the courts in establishing guidelines for adequacy of treatment. The response of institutional psychiatry has been less than enthusiastic, and that of psychology, nonexistent. That we were not invited should by no means keep us from filling this vacuum.

Jurists are acutely aware of their "layman" status in attempting to understand the peculiar complexities of mental illness and have thus turned to what has all too often been the pallid assistance of psychiatry for expert guidance. Yet, a courageous few have struck out on their own, and perhaps the best known of such instances is the landmark decision of Judge [Frank Minis]

Johnson [Jr.] in *Wyatt v. Stickney* [1971]. Here the court held that civilly committed patients had a right to treatment and, with the guidance of psychiatric and psychological experts, ordered sweeping changes in the Alabama state hospital system. Less widely recognized is that in the same year, in a similar suit by the patients of the Georgia state hospital system, the court in *Burnham v. Department of Public Health* held that there was no such right and, further, that courts were not equipped to meddle in such issues as adequacy of treatment, since they lacked the medical expertise. Clearly, what was needed at this point was a ruling by the Supreme Court on the constitutionality of the alleged right to treatment. It came in *O'Connor v. Donaldson* when the Court held,

> The fact that state law may have authorized confinement of the *harmless* mentally ill does not in itself establish a constitutionally adequate purpose for the confinement.

And further,

> A finding of "mental illness" alone cannot justify locking up a person against his will in simple custodial confinement . . . *if they are dangerous to no one*, and can live safely in freedom.

"Dangerous" and "Treatment" Must Be Clarified

Note that the Court did not confront the question of the right of the state to confine a dangerous individual without providing adequate treatment. Actually, *O'Connor* never raised this question, as Donaldson's physicians had admitted that he was not dangerous. The narrowness of this decision is thus not surprising, as the Supreme Court traditionally avoids dealing with more issues than are presented in the case before it. Whether or not a dangerous patient also has a right to treatment awaits another decision at another time. What is far more important is that the Supreme Court did not provide standards for "adequate treatment" or for separating the nondangerous from the dangerous patient. Since treatment must be provided for the former, but (at least for the present) not for the latter, this distinction becomes critical when the lower courts make commitment decisions. The behavioral sciences are in a position to make a truly significant contribution to our society by helping to clarify just what the words *dangerous* and *treatment* actually mean. Even here we would not be blazing entirely new ground, as the way has already been pointed out by the courts in a few cases.

The significance of the term *dangerous* can be illustrated by a simple hypothetical example: If a given court were to decree that every patient it commits is dangerous, in the present state of the law this might well preclude the necessity of providing treatment for any of them. At present, the courts are forced to rely on the expert testimony of the psychiatrist (or more often, the nonpsychiatric physician) to determine whether or not a patient is dangerous. The courts are by no means blind to how casually such prognostications are often realized, but they do not see any clear alternatives to using medical testimony. Bazelon has noted:

> The agency or court responsible for commitments typically contents itself with vague statements from a psychiatrist who has conducted a cursory examination that the individual "could be" or "might be" dangerous. The awesome uncertainty about dangerousness reflected in such language is tolerated on the rationalization that the person is not being imprisoned, but rather hospitalized for treatment. Of course when no treatment is forthcoming, we cluck sympathetically, but reluctantly refuse to release the individual because he is dangerous. Such chicanery is intolerable.

This perceptive jurist has neatly summed up what is probably the usual process by which individuals are committed. This is even more appalling when it is recognized that most commitment hearings are held by fairly low-level state courts, which may well be less diligent in their concern for the individual's rights than is the more sophisticated federal judiciary. Again, what is needed by these courts is guidelines from the Supreme Court, but even the Supreme Court is not omniscient, and assistance from the behavioral sciences could be invaluable to it. It should be recalled that psychologist Kenneth Clark's experiments with dolls were cited by that Court as a source of its reasoning when it overturned public school segregation in *Brown v. Board of Education*.

Psychology Could Better Define "Dangerous" than Psychiatry

There is empirical evidence that psychiatric predictions of dangerousness leave much to be desired. [Lawyer, professor, and politician commentator Alan] Dershowitz reported a survey of the literature in which he determined that

> Psychiatrists are rather inaccurate predictors—inaccurate in an absolute sense—and even less accurate when compared with other professionals such as psychologists, social workers, and correctional officials.

Perhaps the most compelling evidence of how inept the experts are at predicting dangerousness is reported by [attorneys Bruce J.] Ennis and [Loren] Siegel. They note that the Supreme Court in *Baxstrom v. Herold* [1966] held that patients in two maximum-security institutions in New York were not receiving treatment comparable to that available in other institutions throughout the state. Over staff predictions of catastrophe, they ordered that these "violent" patients be distributed throughout these other hospitals. As a result, over 1,000 such "dangerous" patients were transferred. After 1 year, only seven of them had actually manifested violent behavior sufficient to warrant their being returned to maximum security, demonstrating that the staff had overpredicted dangerousness approximately 99% of the time. The simple fact would appear to be that the mental health professions are not very good at making such predictions. When this is coupled with the new-found importance of such predic-

Some argue that the O'Connor v. Donaldson *(1975) ruling was ineffective because it left the lower courts and psychiatrists to determine if individuals with mental illness are dangerous to society. Political commentator Alan Dershowitz was outspoken about psychiatry's inability to predict the dangerousness of certain patients with any objective measures.* © James A. Parcell/ The Washington Post/Getty Images.

tions in deciding whether a patient is entitled to treatment if he or she is to be confined, the issue is clearly drawn. If psychology deserves its self-appointed description as "the science of behavior," it would seem that the gauntlet has been thrown. And even here the courts struggle ahead unaided.

In *In re Balley* [1973], a federal court held that proof of mental illness and dangerousness must be beyond a reasonable doubt. And in *Kendall v. True* [1975], another federal court held that commitment statutes must specify standards by which the courts and their experts can be guided in deciding whether a given individual is in need of confinement. One can only speculate as to where these standards will come from. They could come from empirical research, making the prediction of dangerousness more than the almost mystical exercise of subjective judgment it appears to be at present. Despairing at the apparent inability of psychiatry to provide such guidelines, Dershowitz remarked:

These questions are complex, but this is as it should be, for the business of balancing the liberty of the individual against the risks a free society must tolerate is very complex. That is the business of the law, and these questions need asking and answering.

Again, the contribution the behavioral sciences could make here is obvious, as is the fact that if we fail, the law may well provide its own answers, for better or worse. That this is not idle speculation may be seen in the comments of the court in *Suzuki v. Quisenberry:*

> This court is fully aware of the implications of a return to a "legal model" as opposed to a "medical model" in these cases.

Courts Hesitate to Define Treatment

The courts have been considerably more cautious about attempting to define *treatment* unassisted. Logically enough, since as laymen they view emotional and behavioral disturbances as "illnesses," they have turned to the medical profession for assistance. As noted earlier, this has produced little more than assertions of professional territoriality. However, in view of the holding in *O'Connor v. Donaldson*, it appears that the responsibility for dealing with this issue has been thrust upon them. Thus far, the courts have been hesitant to assert themselves in this area, but the idea of the individual treatment plan mandated in *Wyatt v. Stickney* has begun to spread, since it at least gives the court something to review should a patient complain he or she is receiving inadequate treatment. One suggested standard for judicial review of treatment has been that there should be such a plan, developed by mental health professionals, which a respectable sector of the psychiatric community would agree shows at least some promise of helping the patient. The nature and content of such plans could obviously be enhanced by empirical research into the efficacy of the varied methods of treatment available.

The Behavioral Sciences Could Benefit Mental Health Law

It is not the intent or purpose of this article to presume to program what research should be done; this is a task for many hands. But the courts have opened the doors to long-overdue improvements in the treatment of the mentally ill. Any psychologist who has plied his or her trade in a state institution knows that for far too many patients, such "treatment" is a myth. These people, and the courts who must adjudicate their lives, could benefit immeasurably if the behavioral sciences would turn their concerted attention to the task of empirically defining two words, *dangerous* and *treatment*. Psychiatry has defaulted on its opportunity to contribute significantly in this area. Psychology has the unique orientation toward scholarship and research, as well as the professional skills needed at this point, and it should meet the challenge.

> "My brief was based on the Right to
> Treatment (because I was getting
> no treatment and because I needed
> no treatment, I was entitled to my
> freedom)."

A Man Wrongly Held in an Institution Recounts His Life and His Struggle to Be Released

Personal Narrative

Kenneth Donaldson

In January 1957 Kenneth Donaldson's father placed him in Florida State Hospital in Chattahoochee, Florida, because he thought his son was having paranoid delusions. For the following fifteen years, Kenneth Donaldson remained in the hospital and received no treatment for his supposed psychiatric condition. Throughout his time there, he maintained that he was not mentally ill and petitioned the state and the US Supreme Court repeatedly for his release. In June 1975 the Supreme Court ruled in O'Connor v. Donaldson *that an individual cannot be held in a mental institution if he is able to survive in society and does not present a threat to others. After this ruling, the hospital released Donaldson. In the following viewpoint, which is an excerpt from his book,* Insanity Inside Out, *Donaldson*

Kenneth Donaldson, *Insanity Inside Out.* NY: Crown Publishing, 1976, pp. 134–147.

recounts the steps he took in an effort to secure his release based on his right to treatment, the frustration he felt when this 1960 effort failed, and the mistreatment he and his fellow patients suffered at the hands of the doctors and guards in the hospital.

Day followed monotonous day. From seven to five I sat in the dust of the yard or in a back window or on the porch.

From the window there were suggestions of blue branches in the sun-drenched pines crowding out of the valley a mile away. From a sawmill hidden in haze, a straight plume of smoke cut the horizon, which was as level as a line on the map of Texas.

A quarter-mile below the grilled window of Ward 1, this vast solemnity was cut harmlessly by the school bus and the morning train. The interstate motorist could look up through breaks in the trees, at picturesque white buildings behind chain-link fence, and feel thankful that there was this place for the impossibles.

I noticed the smoke from the sawmill across the valley was diluted by the bright sky. My best plans for three years were like the smoke. But I was still determined to find a way to tell the man feeding logs to the sawmill and the motorist tramping the gas pedal to New Orleans that my flesh and blood differed from theirs only in their possibility of pursuing freedom. . . .

The Right to Treatment Offers an Opportunity for Release

There was a front-page item in *The New York Times* about a new theory advanced (in the *Journal of the American Bar Association*, May 1960) by Brooklyn attorney/medical doctor Morton Birnbaum for the benefit of unjustly held inmates in "mental prisons." He called it the "Right to Treatment." Either the inmate should get treatment or be set free, especially so if no treatment was called for.

I wrote him on May 28: ". . . I hope you are moved to do something . . . I tell my own story, but only because I can tell it better than someone else's. . . . I have been in the presence of doctors

Kenneth Donaldson displays his copy of the US Supreme Court ruling that set him free from the mental institution where he was wrongly held for fifteen years. © Charles Bennett/AP Images.

here for a total of only about 2½ hours in 3½ years. Taking out 1½ hours (dentist, 'psychologist,' admission day and transfer day) there is left one hour spread over 3½ years . . . for what the doctors call 'psychiatric treatment. . . .'"

Doctor Birnbaum's reply enclosed a copy of the bar journal's article and suggested "you use this article as the basis for an application for a writ of habeas corpus [an appearance before a judge] addressed to the Florida Supreme Court. More than this advice I cannot give you as I am not a member of the Florida Bar.". . .

My brief was based on the Right to Treatment (because I was getting no treatment and because I needed no treatment, I was entitled to my freedom) and based on fraud (because the statements on my commitment papers were uniformly untrue).

After the petitions were on their way, I woke to the least sound all night, not unaware that the gestapo could have me on the shitty end of Nine before daybreak, as punishment for the four writs. But, when I got through breakfast in the usual routine, I knew that the worst would not happen before ten days.

Then there was scary news of another sort. May 15 had been our first day in the yard since September 15. When the results of the first annual visit of a mobile X-ray unit were announced, we learned of the incidence of TB [tuberculosis] in four patients and one attendant in the White Male Department alone, the attendant and one patient being on my ward.

On the eleventh day, the writ arrived in my mail. It was dated July 19, a Tuesday. I had now scored for the second time. I could hardly contain myself to whispers as I read to [fellow patients] B & E and Grandma: "The hospital was 'hereby commanded to make return to this Writ instanter, showing the lawful cause and authority for the detention of the petitioner.' Now," I said, "we'll see what they are going to tell the court.". . .

A Possibly Dangerous Man Is Ignored

Two days later, I received from the attorney general's office the respondent's reply to the writ. I was shocked. Doctor O'Connor, as Clinical Director, said I had a "mental disorder which is often found to be chronic and very severe. . . . Most recent psychological examinations reveal that delusional content continues to be in evidence and that a certain senator from Arizona is responsible for the nasty stories being told on him. . . ."

The above is the nub of the entire "medical" case against me.

The respondent's brief included copies of my commitment papers (which I was seeing for the first time) which stated that on December 13, 1956 (which was my third lonely day in the Pinellas County Jail) a sanity committee, appointed by Judge White, consisting of two doctors and one deputy sheriff, had "examined [me] thoroughly both physically and mentally" and found me to be a "schizophrenic paranoiac who was seeing and hearing things and was possibly dangerous to the people of the state." The commitment papers included the information that I had lived in Florida for four years prior to my commitment.

Part II of the respondent's brief is the basis for fifteen succeeding court decisions in my case. It was the defense of *res adjudicata*, relying on an earlier decision. This same court had been intimidated by the hospital in the case of Narrel Damascus [another patient]. If you let this man out, the clinical director had warned of Narrel, we will not be responsible for what happens. Then the court had refused to grant habeas corpus to me in 1957. So that was it, final, for the next decade.

I sent off a rebuttal to the court the next day, via the grapevine. I felt certain that Chief Justice Elwyn Thomas, who had believed my petition, would also believe my rebuttal. Of course, it would be my word against Doctor O'Connor's, but anybody would be able to see that I knew what I was talking about. . . .

On September 15, the mailman hurried up to Ward 1. Jason sent Dixie on the run for me. I opened the letter in front of the attendants but waited till I got to the bed to read:

> . . . the writ of habeas corpus is discharged.

I hadn't believed there could be such cruelty in the United States.

But to be sure, I checked through the grapevine with the court, and the clerk informed me that my rebuttal had not been received. I did not doubt the privilege-card patient, who had put it in the substation letter drop with sufficient postage affixed. Then all the papers I had on the case, which I mailed similarly to Mr. Birnbaum in New York at his request, never showed up in New York. All the demands for an investigation of the hospital's mail-handling to the postal authorities and the court could not make them listen to one who "was seeing and hearing things and was possibly dangerous.". . .

Abuse and Mistreatment Lead to Suicide

While I thought about my next moves, I watched for any openings. Catching Jason smiling one day, I said: "No pile of shit's so big it can't be moved."

Jason's face flushed and his eyes popped. I had him impaled. "Why don't you do something about it then, except talk?" he snapped.

"I have," I said, self-satisfied.

In fact, all of us were doing something. We rallied behind Narrel to bombard the governor to investigate Chattahoochee. Narrel had collected signed statements from each patient who had been tortured. He brought young Jackbrace over to my bed to tell how he had been tied, spread-eagled, on the bed.

"And you mean they actually jumped up and down on you?" I asked.

Jackbrace showed the mark where his belt buckle had cut in.

"Why didn't you report it?" I demanded.

"To who?"

But there were better moments sprinkled about. Grandma came rushing over on a Sunday morning.

"O'Connor did it!" he said. "Shot himself—during the night. I knew he would."

I made him repeat it. By then the whole ward was abuzz, with figures darting from the attendants' station in all directions.

On Monday at 9:00 A.M., Doctor O'Connor came to work as usual. Supervisors and all were disappointed.

The reaction was all the worse, because the men were restless with nervous energy. Here it was the first week in December and no one had been to the yard since October 1, not even ballplayers. The attendants, believing they were on top of the situation, bore down all the more. Two dollars were taken from a letter to Pedro from his mother, though he got the letter. I overheard Gettering: "Donaldson is one of the mammyjammers we're going to get." I didn't mind, for it took attention away from Narrel. I was called down on package run, standing around for an hour, with no package for me after all. The barber took a chunk out of my ear with the clippers. And Jason and Gettering were tearing up and scattering everybody's possessions.

In a night of unrest, one criminal hanged himself in the Flattop and one got out a window from Ward 1. And Sedge yelled out the window at midnight: "You go down to Tallahassee and tell them to come after me."

I thought Sedge was hopelessly funny. I can look back and see he was a tower of strength. From the very heart of a conflagration of noise and brutality, he still had faith that some decent person would listen.

"The jokers are wild," Call Jesstar reported Doctor Gumanis as saying. Our letters brought orders from Tallahassee to close the Flattop. Most of the men came to Ward 1. They told how attendants in the Flattop kept disturbed men awake all night, withheld medication, disclosed the contents of letters the inmates never got, and even threw chicken and bread on the floor, which one had to pick up or go hungry. One man had the fire hose turned on him full force in his cell, three nights in a row. The third night he killed himself. Brother Dean finally prevailed on Gumanis to go talk to the men. For all the good it did, the night after his visit, two more suicided.

Punishment in the name of compassionate medicine.

Feelings of Helplessness in the Face of Death

Carter, who was critical of the attendants' eating all the soup and drinking all the juice intended for the men on sick bay, took a turn for the worse and called me over to the grilled window between sick bay and the poolroom.

"I can hardly stand up, Ken," he said. "Write my sister in Philly. They're doing something to me. I saw them put something in the needle. It wasn't for diabetes."

The new permanent furrows in my brow deepened. Was Carter imagining? Just as he had always stood up for Gumanis, when the rest of us knew the attendants couldn't get away with any more than Gumanis approved of, was Carter wrong again?

"Why don't you tell Gumanis?" I asked.

"They won't let me. I don't even see Mis' Park."

A week later he called me to write again. There was gray in the formerly red face. No replies came to the letters. Eventually, the nurse, in a routine check, learned that he was getting the wrong medication, enough to kill an ox. But he never snapped back. He was withered, stooped, ashen, trembling.

I felt terrible inside. Each of us stood alone, helpless to save ourselves or a friend. It was horror of my total inability to help him that made me avoid the window, but Carter insisted on telling me another story:

"You know Cannonball—the bald-headed chicken plucker. He had a heart attack. Gumanis let him up in a wheelchair. The attendants pushed him under an ice-cold shower. He died in an hour."

Of what value to the world would Cannonball have been, had he lived? Of what value was I to the world? Were all even thousand persons, gathered helter-skelter from around the state— were we all beyond the point of no return? I never slept easy again in Chattahoochee, if I ever had. . . .

Legal Victories Remain the Only Hope for Change

The rest of us kept bombarding the Tampa *Tribune*. Finally, some of our letters appeared on the front page. They told it all. I liked this one: "You could read a newspaper held six inches under the surface of the milk."

Superintendent Rogers allowed a *Tribune* reporter to see one ward of bedridden men, Ward 10. The story told of "the stench of urine," the lack of equipment, the shortage of nurses. The public demanded an investigation.

That same week, Narrel introduced Happotine: "He just came up from the Flattop, Ken. I told him he could trust you."

Happotine refused to shake hands. He refused to say anything. Narrel said wait. Happotine was not a beast. His crimes were armed robbery and safecracking. He came back the third day and studied me, with narrowed eyes withdrawn in his fine-lined prison pallor. The fourth day he told me he had been in prisons and asylums all over the country.

"I led riots in Missouri and West Virginia," he said. "This place is ripe."

"These men won't stick together," I said. "They go all which ways."

"Give me six men—that's all I need."

"Innocent men would get killed."

"You've got to shake this state up."

Narrel advocated caution too. At least two attendants would get killed initially, if we tore the place up.

"So what?" Happotine said. "Many an innocent man died at the Bastille."

But after riots, after the broken bones are mended, public indignation gives way to the gray mold of indifference again. If we could accomplish a legal victory, then there would be enough legal antibiotics to keep things pure. The men listened to Narrel and me.

> "We confront the question whether the
> proscription of discrimination may
> require placement of persons with
> mental disabilities in community
> settings rather than in institutions."

Individuals with Mental Disabilities Have the Right to Live in a Community Instead of an Institution

The Supreme Court's Decision

Ruth Bader Ginsburg

In the following viewpoint, the US Supreme Court finds that under Title II of the Americans with Disabilities Act of 1990, confining an individual to an institutional setting for treatment, when a community setting could better meet their needs, is discrimination. Thus, the court rules that if mental-health professionals determine an individual's needs can be met in a community-based setting, the individual in question prefers the community to the institution, and the placement does not place undue burden on the states, then an individual with a mental disability must receive treatment in a community-based program. Appointed by President Bill Clinton, Ruth Bader Ginsburg has served on the Supreme Court since 1993.

Ruth Bader Ginsburg, Opinion of the Court, *Olmstead v. LC and EW*, US Supreme Court, June 22, 1999.

Before serving on the court, Ginsburg worked to advance women's rights.

This case concerns the proper construction of the anti-discrimination provision contained in the public services portion (Title II) of the Americans with Disabilities Act [ADA] of 1990. Specifically, we confront the question whether the proscription of discrimination may require placement of persons with mental disabilities in community settings rather than in institutions. The answer, we hold, is a qualified yes. Such action is in order when the State's treatment professionals have determined that community placement is appropriate, the transfer from institutional care to a less restrictive setting is not opposed by the affected individual, and the placement can be reasonably accommodated, taking into account the resources available to the State and the needs of others with mental disabilities. In so ruling, we affirm the decision of the Eleventh Circuit in substantial part. We remand the case, however, for further consideration of the appropriate relief, given the range of facilities the State maintains for the care and treatment of persons with diverse mental disabilities, and its obligation to administer services with an even hand.

The ADA Protects Against Discrimination

This case, as it comes to us, presents no constitutional question. The complaints filed by plaintiffs-respondents L.C. and E.W. did include such an issue; L.C. and E.W. alleged that defendants-petitioners, Georgia health care officials, failed to afford them minimally adequate care and freedom from undue restraint, in violation of their rights under the Due Process Clause of the Fourteenth Amendment. But neither the District Court nor the Court of Appeals reached those Fourteenth Amendment claims. Instead, the courts below resolved the case solely on statutory grounds. Our review is similarly confined. Mindful that it is a

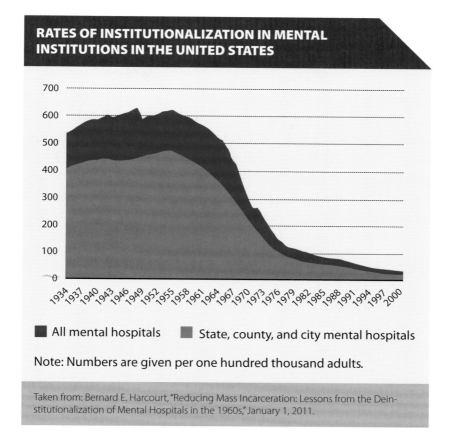

RATES OF INSTITUTIONALIZATION IN MENTAL INSTITUTIONS IN THE UNITED STATES

■ All mental hospitals   ■ State, county, and city mental hospitals

Note: Numbers are given per one hundred thousand adults.

Taken from: Bernard E. Harcourt, "Reducing Mass Incarceration: Lessons from the Deinstitutionalization of Mental Hospitals in the 1960s," January 1, 2011.

statute we are construing, we set out first the legislative and regulatory prescriptions on which the case turns.

In the opening provisions of the ADA, Congress stated findings applicable to the statute in all its parts. Most relevant to this case, Congress determined that

> (2) historically, society has tended to isolate and segregate individuals with disabilities, and, despite some improvements, such forms of discrimination against individuals with disabilities continue to be a serious and pervasive social problem;
> (3) discrimination against individuals with disabilities persists in such critical areas as . . . institutionalization . . . ;

(5) individuals with disabilities continually encounter various forms of discrimination, including outright intentional exclusion, . . . failure to make modifications to existing facilities and practices, . . . [and] segregation . . . .

Congress then set forth prohibitions against discrimination in employment (Title I, §§12111–12117), public services furnished by governmental entities (Title II, §§12131–12165), and public accommodations provided by private entities (Title III, §§12181–12189). The statute as a whole is intended "to provide a clear and comprehensive national mandate for the elimination of discrimination against individuals with disabilities."

This case concerns Title II, the public services portion of the ADA. The provision of Title II centrally at issue reads:

Subject to the provisions of this subchapter, no qualified individual with a disability shall, by reason of such disability, be excluded from participation in or be denied the benefits of the services, programs, or activities of a public entity, or be subjected to discrimination by any such entity.

Title II's definition section states that "public entity" includes "any State or local government," and "any department, agency, [or] special purpose district." The same section defines "qualified individual with a disability" as

an individual with a disability who, with or without reasonable modifications to rules, policies, or practices, the removal of architectural, communication, or transportation barriers, or the provision of auxiliary aids and services, meets the essential eligibility requirements for the receipt of services or the participation in programs or activities provided by a public entity. . . .

We recite these regulations with the caveat that we do not here determine their validity. While the parties differ on the proper construction and enforcement of the regulations, we do not understand petitioners to challenge the regulatory formulations themselves as outside the congressional authorization. . . .

The Resources and Obligations of the State

Endeavoring to carry out Congress' instruction to issue regulations implementing Title II, the Attorney General, in the integration and reasonable-modifications regulations, made two key determinations. The first concerned the scope of the ADA's discrimination proscription, the second concerned the obligation of the States to counter discrimination. As to the first, the Attorney General concluded that unjustified placement or retention of persons in institutions, severely limiting their exposure to the outside community, constitutes a form of discrimination based on disability prohibited by Title II. Regarding the States' obligation to avoid unjustified isolation of individuals with disabilities, the Attorney General provided that States could resist modifications that "would fundamentally alter the nature of the service, program, or activity."

The Court of Appeals essentially upheld the Attorney General's construction of the ADA. As just recounted, the appeals court ruled that the unjustified institutionalization of persons with mental disabilities violated Title II; the court then remanded with instructions to measure the cost of caring for L.C. and E.W. in a community-based facility against the State's mental health budget.

We affirm the Court of Appeals' decision in substantial part. Unjustified isolation, we hold, is properly regarded as discrimination based on disability. But we recognize, as well, the States' need to maintain a range of facilities for the care and treatment of persons with diverse mental disabilities, and the States' obligation to administer services with an even hand. Accordingly, we further hold that the Court of Appeals' remand instruction was unduly restrictive. In evaluating a State's fundamental-alteration defense, the District Court must consider, in view of

Lives Improve with Community-Based Treatment

The lives of the two *Olmstead* plaintiffs, Ms. Curtis [L.C.] and Ms. Wilson [E.W.], illustrate the benefit and magnitude of the decision and show the positive effect the decision can have on individuals as well as society as a whole. Ms. Curtis and Ms. Wilson progressed rapidly once they were moved to community-based settings. Their rapid advancements revealed the limitations of their former institutional circumstances. Ms. Curtis takes long walks and has reconnected with her mother and sister. She visits the mall, picks out her own clothes, and has learned to plan a menu. Additionally, she speaks clearly, communicates well, and has developed meaningful friendships with others that live with her in a group home. With practical assistance and encouragement from her customized support team, Ms. Curtis has started to produce and sell note cards that illustrate her own artwork.

Ms. Wilson spent a year in a group home where she decorated her own room and organized picture albums. She then transitioned into a home where she lived with a caretaker and a friend. Ms. Wilson attended a prevocational program and became increasingly independent. Interestingly, she took complete responsibility for her own medical needs, which was one domain in which institutional doctors felt she could not succeed independently.

Samantha A. DiPolito, "Olmstead v. L.C.— Deinstitutionalization and Community Integration: An Awakening of the Nation's Conscience?," Mercer Law Review, *vol. 58, 2007.*

the resources available to the State, not only the cost of providing community-based care to the litigants, but also the range of services the State provides others with mental disabilities, and the State's obligation to mete out those services equitably.

Segregation of People with Disabilities Is Discrimination

We examine first whether, as the Eleventh Circuit held, undue institutionalization qualifies as discrimination "by reason of . . . disability." The Department of Justice has consistently advocated that it does. Because the Department is the agency directed by Congress to issue regulations implementing Title II, its views warrant respect. . . .

The State argues that L.C. and E.W. encountered no discrimination "by reason of" their disabilities because they were not denied community placement on account of those disabilities. Nor were they subjected to "discrimination," the State contends, because "'discrimination' necessarily requires uneven treatment of similarly situated individuals," and L.C. and E.W. had identified no comparison class, *i.e.*, no similarly situated individuals given preferential treatment. We are satisfied that Congress had a more comprehensive view of the concept of discrimination advanced in the ADA.

The ADA stepped up earlier measures to secure opportunities for people with developmental disabilities to enjoy the benefits of community living. The Developmentally Disabled Assistance and Bill of Rights Act (DDABRA), a 1975 measure, stated in aspirational terms that "[t]he treatment, services, and habilitation for a person with developmental disabilities . . . *should be* provided in the setting that is least restrictive of the person's personal liberty." In a related legislative endeavor, the Rehabilitation Act of 1973, Congress used mandatory language to proscribe discrimination against persons with disabilities. Ultimately, in the ADA, enacted in 1990, Congress not only required all public entities to refrain from discrimination, additionally, in findings applicable to the entire statute, Congress explicitly identified unjustified "segregation" of persons with disabilities as a "for[m] of discrimination."

Recognition that unjustified institutional isolation of persons with disabilities is a form of discrimination reflects two evident judgments. First, institutional placement of persons who can handle and benefit from community settings perpetuates unwarranted assumptions that persons so isolated are incapable or unworthy of participating in community life. Second, confinement in an institution severely diminishes the everyday life activities of individuals, including family relations, social contacts, work options, economic independence, educational advancement, and cultural enrichment. Dissimilar treatment correspondingly exists in this key respect: In order to receive needed medical services, persons with mental disabilities must, because of those disabilities, relinquish participation in community life they could enjoy given reasonable accommodations, while persons without mental disabilities can receive the medical services they need without similar sacrifice.

Professionals Determine Eligibility

The State urges that, whatever Congress may have stated as its findings in the ADA, the Medicaid statute "reflected a congressional policy preference for treatment in the institution over treatment in the community." The State correctly used the past tense. Since 1981, Medicaid has provided funding for state-run home and community-based care through a waiver program. Indeed, the United States points out that the Department of Health and Human Services (HHS) "has a policy of encouraging States to take advantage of the waiver program, and often approves more waiver slots than a State ultimately uses."

We emphasize that nothing in the ADA or its implementing regulations condones termination of institutional settings for persons unable to handle or benefit from community settings. Title II provides only that "qualified individual[s] with a disability" may not "be subjected to discrimination." "Qualified individuals," the ADA further explains, are persons with disabilities who, "with or without reasonable modifications to rules, policies, or practices, . . . mee[t] the essential eligibility requirements for the receipt of services or the participation in programs or activities provided by a public entity."

In the 1999 case of Olmstead v. L.C. and E.W., *US Supreme Court Justice Ruth Bader Ginsberg ruled that confining an individual to an institution when a community setting is more suitable is discriminatory.* © J. Scott Applewhite/AP Images.

Consistent with these provisions, the State generally may rely on the reasonable assessments of its own professionals in determining whether an individual "meets the essential eligibility requirements" for habilitation in a community-based program. Absent such qualification, it would be inappropriate to remove a patient from the more restrictive setting. Nor is there any federal requirement that community-based treatment be imposed on patients who do not desire it. In this case, however, there is no genuine dispute concerning the status of L.C. and E.W. as individuals "qualified" for noninstitutional care: The State's own professionals determined that community-based treatment would be appropriate for L.C. and E.W., and neither woman opposed such treatment.

The State Must Have Leeway in Managing Resources

The State's responsibility, once it provides community-based treatment to qualified persons with disabilities, is not boundless. The reasonable-modifications regulation speaks of "reasonable modifications" to avoid discrimination, and allows States to resist modifications that entail a "fundamenta[l] alter[ation]" of the States' services and programs. The Court of Appeals construed this regulation to permit a cost-based defense "only in the most limited of circumstances," and remanded to the District Court to consider, among other things, "whether the additional expenditures necessary to treat L.C. and E.W. in community-based care would be unreasonable given the demands of the State's mental health budget."

The Court of Appeals' construction of the reasonable-modifications regulation is unacceptable for it would leave the State virtually defenseless once it is shown that the plaintiff is qualified for the service or program she seeks. If the expense entailed in placing one or two people in a community-based treatment program is properly measured for reasonableness against the State's entire mental health budget, it is unlikely that a State, relying on the fundamental-alteration defense, could ever prevail. Sensibly construed, the fundamental-alteration component of the reasonable-modifications regulation would allow the State to show that, in the allocation of available resources, immediate relief for the plaintiffs would be inequitable, given the responsibility the State has undertaken for the care and treatment of a large and diverse population of persons with mental disabilities.

When it granted summary judgment for plaintiffs in this case, the District Court compared the cost of caring for the plaintiffs in a community-based setting with the cost of caring for them in an institution. That simple comparison showed that community placements cost less than institutional confinements. As the United States recognizes, however, a comparison so simple overlooks costs the State cannot avoid; most notably, a "State . . . may experience increased overall expenses by funding community placements without being able to take advantage of the savings associated with the closure of institutions."

As already observed, the ADA is not reasonably read to impel States to phase out institutions, placing patients in need of close care at risk. Nor is it the ADA's mission to drive States to move institutionalized patients into an inappropriate setting, such as a homeless shelter, a placement the State proposed, then retracted, for E.W. Some individuals, like L.C. and E.W. in prior years, may need institutional care from time to time "to stabilize acute psychiatric symptoms." For other individuals, no placement outside the institution may ever be appropriate.

To maintain a range of facilities and to administer services with an even hand, the State must have more leeway than the courts below understood the fundamental-alteration defense to allow. If, for example, the State were to demonstrate that it had a comprehensive, effectively working plan for placing qualified persons with mental disabilities in less restrictive settings, and a waiting list that moved at a reasonable pace not controlled by the State's endeavors to keep its institutions fully populated, the reasonable-modifications standard would be met. In such circumstances, a court would have no warrant effectively to order displacement of persons at the top of the community-based treatment waiting list by individuals lower down who commenced civil actions.

States Must Provide Community-Based Treatment

For the reasons stated, we conclude that, under Title II of the ADA, States are required to provide community-based treatment for persons with mental disabilities when the State's treatment professionals determine that such placement is appropriate, the affected persons do not oppose such treatment, and the placement can be reasonably accommodated, taking into account the resources available to the State and the needs of others with mental disabilities. The judgment of the Eleventh Circuit is therefore affirmed in part and vacated in part, and the case is remanded for further proceedings consistent with this opinion.

8

> "The District of Columbia shall provide
> suitable publicly supported education
> regardless of the degree of the child's
> mental, physical or emotional disability
> or impairment."

Students Have the Right to Receive a Free Public Education Regardless of Disability or Cost

The Circuit Court's Decision

Joseph Cornelius Waddy

In 1972 seven special-needs children sued the District of Columbia (DC) education system in Mills v. Board of Education of the District of Columbia *for denying them their right to a free public education. The DC school board would not allow the children to attend classes on the grounds that their conditions prevented them from being educated in the public schools, and alternative education would be too costly for the school board to provide. In the following viewpoint, which is his ruling, Judge Joseph Cornelius Waddy finds that the board of education's decision not to let the special-needs children attend school violates not only the school board's own stated statutes on the right, but also US Supreme Court*

Joseph Cornelius Waddy, Opinion of the Court, *Mills v. Board of Education of District of Columbia*, August 1, 1972.

rulings that guarantee American children the right to a free public education. Thus, Waddy rules in favor of the plaintiffs, calling for their admittance into the DC public schools and establishing guidelines to ensure that all children in the future are allowed to attend school, regardless of their condition or the cost of accommodation. Joseph Cornelius Waddy served as judge for the US District Court for the District of Columbia from 1967 until his death in 1978.

This is a civil action brought on behalf of seven children of school age by their next friends in which they seek a declaration of rights and to enjoin the defendants from excluding them from the District of Columbia Public Schools and/or denying them publicly supported education and to compel the defendants to provide them with immediate and adequate education and educational facilities in the public schools or alternative placement at public expense. They also seek additional and ancillary relief to effectuate the primary relief. They allege that although they can profit from an education either in regular classrooms with supportive services or in special classes adopted to their needs, they have been labelled as behavioral problems, mentally retarded, emotionally disturbed or hyperactive, and denied admission to the public schools or excluded therefrom after admission, with no provision for alternative educational placement or periodic review. . . .

The Board Is Violating Its Own Statutes

Plaintiffs' entitlement to relief in this case is clear. The applicable statutes and regulations and the Constitution of the United States require it.

Section 31-201 of the District of Columbia Code requires that:

> Every parent, guardian, or other person residing [permanently or temporarily] in the District of Columbia who has custody or control of a child between the ages of seven and

sixteen years shall cause said child to be regularly instructed in a public school or in a private or parochial school or instructed privately during the period of each year in which the public schools of the District of Columbia are in session . . .

Under Section 31-203, a child may be "excused" from attendance only when

> . . . upon examination ordered by . . . [the Board of Education of the District of Columbia], [the child] is found to be unable mentally or physically to profit from attendance at school: Provided, however, That if such examination shows that such child may benefit from specialized instruction adapted to his needs, he shall attend upon such instruction.

Failure of a parent to comply with Section 31-201 constitutes a criminal offense. The Court need not belabor the fact that requiring parents to see that their children attend school under pain of criminal penalties presupposes that an educational opportunity will be made available to the children. The Board of Education is required to make such opportunity available. It has adopted rules and regulations consonant with the statutory direction. Chapter XIII of the Board Rules contains the following:

> 1.1—All children of the ages hereinafter prescribed who are bona fide residents of the District of Columbia are entitled to admission and free tuition in the Public Schools of the District of Columbia, subject to the rules, regulations, and orders of the Board of Education and the applicable statutes.
>
> 14.1—Every parent, guardian, or other person residing permanently or temporarily in the District of Columbia who has custody or control of a child residing in the District of Columbia between the ages of seven and sixteen years shall cause said child to be regularly instructed in a public school or in a private or parochial school or instructed privately during the period of each year in which the Public Schools of the District of Columbia are in session, provided that instruction

The 1972 decision of Mills v. Board of Education of District of Columbia *mandated that children cannot be denied public education due to disability.* © Shaun Lowe/E+/Getty Images.

given in such private or parochial school, or privately, is deemed reasonably equivalent by the Board of Education to the instruction given in the Public Schools.

14.3—The Board of Education of the District of Columbia may, upon written recommendation of the Superintendent of Schools, issue a certificate excusing from attendance at school a child who, upon examination by the Department of Pupil Appraisal, Study and Attendance or by the Department of Public Health of the District of Columbia, is found to be unable mentally or physically to profit from attendance at school: Provided, however, that if such examination shows that such child may benefit from specialized instruction adapted to his needs, he shall be required to attend such classes.

Thus the Board of Education has an obligation to provide whatever specialized instruction that will benefit the child. By failing to provide plaintiffs and their class the publicly supported specialized education to which they are entitled, the Board of Education violates the above statutes and its own regulations.

All Children Must Have Access to an Equal Education

The Supreme Court in *Brown v. Board of Education* (1954) stated:

> Today, education is perhaps the most important function of state and local governments. Compulsory school attendance laws and the great expenditures for education both demonstrate our recognition of the importance of education to our democratic society. It is required in the performance of our most basic public responsibilities, even service in the armed forces. It is the very foundation of good citizenship. Today it is a principal instrument in awakening the child to cultural values, in preparing him for later professional training, and in helping him to adjust normally to his environment. In these days, it is doubtful that any child may reasonably be expected to succeed in life if he is denied the opportunity of an education. Such an opportunity, where the state has undertaken to provide it, is a right which must be made available to all on equal terms.

Bolling v. Sharpe, decided the same day as *Brown*, applied the *Brown* rationale to the District of Columbia public schools by finding that:

> Segregation in public education is not reasonably related to any proper governmental objective, and thus it imposes on Negro children of the District of Columbia a burden that constitutes an arbitrary deprivation of their liberty in violation of the Due Process Clause.

In *Hobson v. Hansen* (1967), Circuit Judge J. Skelly Wright considered the pronouncements of the Supreme Court in the intervening years and stated that ". . . the Court has found the due process clause of the Fourteenth Amendment elastic enough to embrace not only the First and Fourth Amendments, but the self-incrimination clause of the Fifth, the speedy trial, confrontation and assistance of counsel clauses of the Sixth, and the cruel and unusual clause of the Eighth." Judge Wright concluded

"From these considerations the court draws the conclusion that the doctrine of equal educational opportunity—the equal protection clause in its application to public school education—is in its full sweep a component of due process binding on the District under the due process clause of the Fifth Amendment."

In *Hobson v. Hansen*, Judge Wright found that denying poor public school children educational opportunities equal to that available to more affluent public school children was violative of the Due Process Clause of the Fifth Amendment. A fortiori, the defendants' conduct here, denying plaintiffs and their class not just an equal publicly supported education but all publicly supported education while providing such education to other children, is violative of the Due Process Clause.

Not only are plaintiffs and their class denied the publicly supported education to which they are entitled many are suspended or expelled from regular schooling or specialized instruction or reassigned without any prior hearing and are given no periodic review thereafter. Due process of law requires a hearing prior to exclusion, termination of classification into a special program. . . .

Cost Is Not an Excuse

The Answer of the defendants to the Complaint contains the following:

> These defendants say that it is impossible to afford plaintiffs the relief they request unless:
>
> (a) The Congress of the United States appropriates millions of dollars to improve special education services in the District of Columbia; or
>
> (b) These defendants divert millions of dollars from funds already specifically appropriated for other educational services in order to improve special educational services. These defendants suggest that to do so would violate an Act of Congress and would be inequitable to children outside the alleged plaintiff class.

This Court is not persuaded by that contention.

The defendants are required by the Constitution of the United States, the District of Columbia Code, and their own regulations to provide a publicly supported education for these "exceptional" children. Their failure to fulfill this clear duty to include and retain these children in the public school system, or otherwise provide them with publicly supported education, and their failure to afford them due process hearing and periodical review, cannot be excused by the claim that there are insufficient funds. In *Goldberg v. Kelly* (1969), the Supreme Court, in a case that involved the right of a welfare recipient to a hearing before termination of his benefits, held that Constitutional rights must be afforded citizens despite the greater expense involved. The Court stated that "the State's interest that his [welfare recipient] payments not be erroneously terminated, clearly outweighs the State's competing concern to prevent any increase in its fiscal and administrative burdens." Similarly the District of Columbia's interest in educating the excluded children clearly must outweigh its interest in preserving its financial resources. If sufficient funds are not available to finance all of the services and programs that are needed and desirable in the system then the available funds must be expended equitably in such a manner that no child is entirely excluded from a publicly supported education consistent with his needs and ability to benefit therefrom. The inadequacies of the District of Columbia Public School System whether occasioned by insufficient funding or administrative inefficiency, certainly cannot be permitted to bear more heavily on the "exceptional" or handicapped child than on the normal child. . . .

All Children Must Receive a Free Public Education

Plaintiffs having filed their verified complaint seeking an injunction and declaration of rights as set forth more fully in the verified complaint and the prayer for relief contained therein;

and having moved this Court for summary judgment . . . it is hereby ordered, adjudged and decreed that summary judgment in favor of plaintiffs and against defendants be, and hereby is, granted, and judgment is entered in this action as follows: 1. That no child eligible for a publicly supported education in the District of Columbia public schools shall be excluded from a regular public school assignment by a Rule, policy, or practice of the Board of Education of the District of Columbia or its agents unless such child is provided (a) adequate alternative educational services suited to the child's needs, which may include special education or tuition grants, and (b) a constitutionally adequate prior hearing and periodic review of the child's status, progress, and the adequacy of any educational alternative. . . .

The District of Columbia shall provide to each child of school age a free and suitable publicly supported education regardless of the degree of the child's mental, physical or emotional disability or impairment. Furthermore, defendants shall not exclude any child resident in the District of Columbia from such publicly supported education on the basis of a claim of insufficient resources.

Defendants shall not suspend a child from the public schools for disciplinary reasons for any period in excess of two days without affording him a hearing . . . and without providing for his education during the period of any such suspension.

Professionals Will Determine an Appropriate Education Plan

Defendants shall provide each identified member of plaintiff class with a publicly supported education suited to his needs within thirty (30) days of the entry of this order. With regard to children who later come to the attention of any defendant, within twenty (20) days after he becomes known, the evaluation (case study approach) . . . shall be completed and within 30 days after completion of the evaluation, placement shall be made so as

The Importance of Parental Involvement

President Gerald Ford signed the Education for All Handicapped Children Act (EAHCA) into law in 1975. Since the original passage of the EAHCA, the law has been amended four times and renamed the Individuals with Disabilities Education Act (IDEA). After each revision, the U.S. Department of Education has issued new regulations implementing the Act. The current IDEA, as amended, is codified in Title 20 of the United States Code.

When the EAHCA was being written, the law's authors recognized the importance of parents being involved in the development of their child's program of special education. In fact, parental involvement has been one of the cornerstones of the law. In 2004 Congress emphasized the necessity of meaningful parental involvement in the IDEA'S findings and purpose section:

> Almost 30 years of research and experience has demonstrated that the education of children with disabilities can be made more effective by—strengthening the role and responsibility of parents and ensuring that families of such children have meaningful opportunities to participate in the education of their children at school and at home.

Congress believed that access to a free appropriate public education (FAPE) for students with disabilities in part depended on their parents' ability to advocate on their child's behalf. One purpose of the EAHCA, therefore, was to create specific procedural safeguards for parents to ensure that their children would receive a FAPE.

Terrye Conroy, Mitchell L. Yell, Antonis Katsiyannis, and Terri S. Collins, "The U.S. Supreme Court and Parental Rights Under the Individuals with Disabilities Education Act," Focus on Exceptional Children, October 2010.

to provide the child with a publicly supported education suited to his needs. . . .

Defendants shall utilize public or private agencies to evaluate the educational needs of all identified "exceptional" children and, within twenty (20) days of the entry of this order, shall file with the Clerk of this Court their proposal for each individual placement in a suitable educational program, including the provision of compensatory educational services where required.

Defendants, within twenty (20) days of the entry of this order, shall, also submit such proposals to each parent or guardian of such child, respectively, along with a notification that if they object to such proposed placement within a period of time to be fixed by the parties or by the Court, they may have their objection heard by a Hearing Officer. . . .

Parents Must Be Informed of Their Children's Placement

a. Each member of the plaintiff class is to be provided with a publicly supported educational program suited to his needs, within the context of a presumption that among the alternative programs of education, placement in a regular public school class with appropriate ancillary services is preferable to placement in a special school class.

b. Before placing a member of the class in such a program, defendants shall notify his parent or guardian of the proposed educational placement, the reasons therefore, and the right to a hearing before a Hearing Officer if there is an objection to the placement proposed. . . .

c. Hereinafter, children who are residents of the District of Columbia and are thought by any of the defendants, or by officials, parents or guardians, to be in need of a program of special education, shall neither be placed in, transferred from or to, nor denied placement in such a program unless defendants shall have first notified their parents or guardians of such proposed placement, transfer or denial, the reasons therefore, and of the right to a hearing before a Hearing Officer if there is an objection to the placement, transfer or denial of placement. . . .

d. Defendants shall not, on grounds of discipline, cause the exclusion, suspension, expulsion, postponement, inter-school transfer, or any other denial of access to regular instruction in the public schools to any child for more than two days without first notifying the child's parent or guardian of such proposed action, the reasons therefore, and of the hearing before a Hearing Officer. . . .

Children's Punishment Must Be Limited

Pending the hearing and receipt of notification of the decision, there shall be no change in the child's educational placement unless the principal (responsible to the Superintendent) shall warrant that the continued presence of the child in his current program would endanger the physical well-being of himself or others. In such exceptional cases, the principal shall be responsible for ensuring that the child receives some form of educational assistance and/or diagnostic examination during the interim period prior to the hearing.

No finding that disciplinary action is warranted shall be made unless the Hearing Officer first finds, by clear and convincing evidence, that the child committed a prohibited act upon which the proposed disciplinary action is based. After this finding has been made, the Hearing Officer shall take such disciplinary action as he shall deem appropriate. This action shall not be more severe than that recommended by the school official initiating the suspension proceedings.

No suspension shall continue for longer than ten (10) school days after the date of the hearing, or until the end of the school year, whichever comes first. In such cases, the principal (responsible to the Superintendent) shall be responsible for ensuring that the child receives some form of educational assistance and/or diagnostic examination during the suspension period.

"*[The Individuals with Disabilities Education Act] reflects and perpetuates the very duality, the very separateness that it seeks to combat.*"

The Reauthorized IDEA Should Mandate an Equal, Integrated Education for All Children

Nina Zuna and Rud Turnbull

In 1990 the Individuals with Disabilities Education Act (IDEA) replaced the Education for All Handicapped Children Act of 1975, the first federal legislation enacted to provide equal rights to education for children with disabilities. IDEA placed more emphasis on the individual than on the individual's condition. In the following viewpoint, written in early 2004 as US Congress considered revising and reauthorizing IDEA, Nina Zuna and Rud Turnbull address the flaws that they believe still plague IDEA and propose that the reauthorized act remove the labels and classifications that they believe limit it from creating truly equal education opportunities for all American students. Zuna and Turnbull maintain that until the public views disability as a natural condition, separation and inequality will continue to exist and prevent students with disabilities from achieving full equality within the education system. Zuna

Nina Zuna and Rud Turnbull, "Imagine All the People, Sharing . . . or a (Not so) Modest Proposal Made on the Eve of the IDEA Reauthorization," *Research and Practice for Persons with Severe Disabilities (RPSD),* vol. 29, no. 3, Fall 2004. Copyright © 2004 by T A S H. All rights reserved. Reproduced by permission.

and Turnbull believe that altering IDEA as they suggest would be one way to initiate this change in perception. Nina Zuna is an assistant professor of special education at the University of Texas at Austin, and Rud Turnbull is a distinguished professor of special education and the codirector of the Beach Center on Disability at the University of Kansas.

From whom should we take our cues as Congress considers the reauthorization of IDEA [the Individuals with Disabilities Education Act]? From [singer, songwriter, and member of the Beatles] John Lennon, imagining that all the students share the schools together? Or from Jonathan Swift (1729), author of *Gulliver's Travels* and the Dean of St. Paul's Cathedral, London, who made an audacious and ironic proposal that the best way to cure hunger in Ireland would be to cannibalize infants, thereby reducing the number of people who clamor for food while simultaneously feeding those who are older and stronger and presumptively more valuable to society than a newborn? Why not take our cues from both, and, in a Swiftian spirit of frontal challenges to convention, make a proposal that, Lennon-like, imagines what Congress might have done in 1975 and should do in 2004?

To begin, let us consider the educational, economic, cultural, and societal implications of IDEA. In a Swiftian spirit of audacity, let us boldly challenge our contemporaries and the system that IDEA created—a system that creates inherently unequal treatment and opportunity even while advocating for equal treatment and opportunity, a system that can be unintentionally maleficent even while purporting to be beneficent. And, Lennon-like, let us share a vision for new education policy and practice for all children. Yes, all. What don't we understand about that simple word "all"?

Separate Educational Environments

No doubt, Congress was right to address the dismal and discriminatory treatment of school-aged students when, in 1975, it enacted IDEA's predecessor law. In retrospect, perhaps our actions were wrong. Perhaps the law and we who advocated for the original law (and its creation of a separate set of rights restricted to students with disabilities) erred grievously in the choice of means. Rather than adopting a universal approach to educating students with disabilities by creating equal rights for both them and students who do not have disabilities, Congress with our approval enacted a separatist, segregating, exceptionalistic approach. In a sense, this decision led to the further separation of children: within the walls of their school, their community, and later as adults, isolates within mainstream society.

The 1975 law was a powerful victory for children with disabilities and their families, and perhaps it was all we as a nation and the children's advocates knew to do at the time, but that law marked the beginning of the formal line of demarcation between general education and special education. It took more than a decade for parents and educators to challenge the separate environments in which their children were educated, to move beyond the civil-rights model of integration into a human-rights model of physical and psychological inclusion, participation, and contribution. By then, however, separation of general and special education was firm. The question, "Who is responsible for the education of a child with a disability, the special educator or the general educator?" had been answered: Those who are so different should be identified and educated by those who are also so differently qualified.

Joint responsibility for the education of children with disabilities both philosophically and in practice does not exist, largely because the 1975 law decreed separatism. The field of special education now is hardly a single system; instead, it is a system of systems, a conglomeration of fragmented services often delivered in isolation from one another and rarely integrated within the general education environment. It is a microcosm of its own programs, research, teachers, instructional practices, and laws.

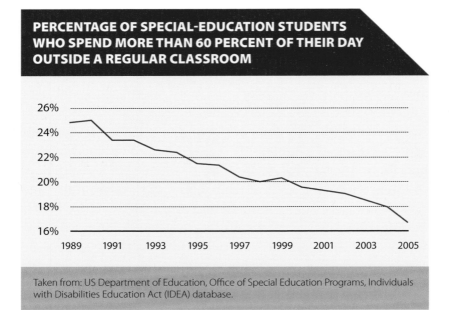

PERCENTAGE OF SPECIAL-EDUCATION STUDENTS WHO SPEND MORE THAN 60 PERCENT OF THEIR DAY OUTSIDE A REGULAR CLASSROOM

Taken from: US Department of Education, Office of Special Education Programs, Individuals with Disabilities Education Act (IDEA) database.

We do not wish to disparage the professionals and schools who have delivered services according to the letter and spirit of the law, because they do exist, but all is not well everywhere. Why is this so? Because in 1973–75, when IDEA was first shaped, we—special educators, lawyers, advocates of all kinds—lacked the foresight to plan for the professional practices necessary to educate all children together. For nearly three decades, many special educators and families have been fighting for and continue to fight for true equality and inclusion for their students. We can only wonder what our educational system and society would be today if, when Lennon was imagining, we had envisioned all teachers would teach all students.

Classification Causes Psychological Harm

In his "Modest Proposal," Swift ironically argued that the proper cure for poverty is for the wealthy to eliminate the poor, literally to consume them. Is it too bold for us now to suggest that IDEA's separatist, specialized, exceptionalistic approach contributes to psychological harm and an unequal education for children with disabilities? It is as though the education system "consumes" its own.

Before 1975, children with disabilities were denied an education solely on the basis of their disabilities. Two court cases, *PARC v. Pennsylvania* (1972) and *Mills v. D.C. Board of Education* (1972), creatively used the precedent of *Brown v. Topeka Board of Education* (1954) to apply the equal protection argument to students with disabilities. *PARC* and *Mills* legitimatized Congressional action in 1975. So far, so good. But *Brown's* factual predicate—separate is inherently unequal because separation teaches those who are separated that they deserve separation and are intrinsically less worthy—was not used to the extent necessary to ensure equal protection and equal opportunity for all children.

It is not enough to read *Brown* by substituting "child with disability" for "Negro," as an equal protection case alone. Read it in a more robust way, a more Swiftian/radical way: substitute "labeling" or "classification" for "segregation," then also substitute "legally equivalent" for "racially integrated." Finally, add a statement that general education students are not labeled. . . .

It is the very act of classification, of labeling, that justified two separate educational policies, one for children with disabilities (IDEA) and one primarily for children without disabilities (NCLB) [the No Child Left Behind Act of 2002]. True, in some children disability (i.e., the extent of disability) is a distinction that does and can make a difference that justifies different treatment, either by way of additional accommodations or unequal but not invidious treatment.

But with respect to so many children now classified into special education, we must return to *Brown's* factual predicate and ask: have we robbed, and do we continue to rob, individuals of their liberty by labeling them with a disability? Do we do a "Swift number" on them? Arguably, yes, because IDEA guarantees special education services only after a child is identified as having a disability.

It is not the evaluation for eligibility or the provision of individualized education that is the problem *per se;* it is the consequences that attach to evaluation—the classification and labeling that categorize, stigmatize, sort, separate, and endure. These consequences, in essence, "consume" their identity. They are no longer just children. They are now, even with our polite "person first" language, children with disabilities. These consequences are further sanctioned by an IDEA reimbursement/financing system that incentivizes labeling. What freedom does the child have not to be labeled? What messages do we, *Brown*-like, send? What have we taught the child? What do we teach others and ourselves in power? What powers do we acquire thereby? The most critical issue in special education, and in all disability policy, is the issue of classification. It is the beginning and end-point, the alpha and omega, of a person's life.

Refusing to Label

Imagine, then, life without a label. Imagine schools that do not label, laws that do not result in labels, and laws and systems that abjure the unequal by abjuring classification. What message would that approach convey? To the (now-labeled) students, it would say, "We refuse to cause you emotional pain, to isolate you, to stigmatize you, and to treat you invidiously, here and after you leave school."

To each of us, the refuse-to-label message would say that we truly understand *Brown*, not as (just) the (great) equal-protection case but as the great admonition against causing harm in the name of doing good, as the clear warning that we with the power to label can hurt those whom we label. The message would also be that we do not want to perpetuate two systems of education, two classes of students, and two types of citizens: those with and those without disabilities. The message would be that IDEA, for

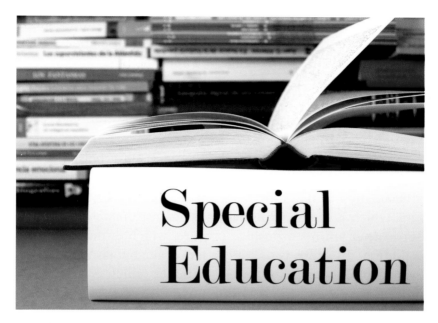

Many have challenged the separation of special education from the rest of the school curriculum, citing its psychological damage on children who are classified as different from everyone else. © Alejandro Dans Neergaard/ShutterStock.com.

all of its power, is fundamentally flawed because, ironically, it reflects and perpetuates the very duality, the very separateness that it seeks to combat.

A refuse-to-label message would say something about us all, which is that each of us lives somewhere on a continuum of disability. None of us is so comely or handsome as to be regarded as "perfect." None of us is so bionic as to be the superman or superwoman, the super-mensch. And each of us, as ADA [the Americans with Disabilities Act] proclaims, must admit that disability is a natural part of the human experience and therefore, as ADA fails to say, each of us who, when "disabled," must be welcomed into society and not simply protected from discrimination. Imagine what message would come if Congress were to have said that disability is a natural experience that is to be accepted, even welcomed, and that those who are "different enough" are to be welcomed, not simply protected. That message, more than any "least restrictive" principle, would have profound implications for the social relationships of children with disabilities when they are in school and when they are not, when they are children and when they are adults.

"Just Accommodate, Do Not Differentiate"

A modest proposal might require a modest start, but let us just imagine something not so modest. Start with changing the ADA proclamation so that it no longer affirms simply a negative posture, which is that discrimination is against the nation's policy, but instead affirms a positive posture, which is that a natural condition, disability, is not only a fact of life but also a welcome fact. Consider adopting, as our national policy, Sweden's approach, which eschews regarding disability as a "characteristic of a person" and instead recognizes the consequence of having a disability: a person with a functional impairment "is confronted by an inaccessible environment.". . .

Imagine the power of reversing our policies by adopting these (im)modest proposals. Enact a single federal education law: "Free Appropriate Public Education for All." Hold every student to "high expectations." To implement that affirming posture, adopt universally designed curricula, train teachers to work collaboratively with each other to serve all students, stop calling some of them "general" and others "special" educators (for labeling them is deleterious to our ends, just as labeling students is), open up "resource rooms" to serve the continuum of needs of all students, and blend (or braid) the exceptionalistic funding streams with the universalistic ones. Incorporate and fund related services and supplementary aids and services in such a way that it benefits not only those students who qualify for additional services but also struggling students who may not qualify. Then, do as most families (i.e., as microcosms of society do) do: treat the member with the "disability/impairment" as a "regular" member of the family, not as a "special" member who needs unusually solicitous attention for every minute detail of his or her life. Just accommodate, do not differentiate.

Conduct for all children—those we now call "special" and those we regard as "regular" (in the sense that "regular" education teachers instruct them in the "general curriculum")—a functional behavioral assessment when their behaviors impede their or others' learning or create unacceptable risks to health and safety, and provide positive behavioral supports to ameliorate challenging behaviors. Extend to all children (remember, "all means all") the right of "no cessation" of education.

Changing Education Will Change Society

Our nation is becoming more and more culturally diverse every year. A "new" (ethnic) minority now outnumbers the "old" one. Our national tongue, while still an Americanized and regionalized English, is more and more polyglot [multilingual] every day. The decennial census form is unfairly bounded by now-outmoded classifications; it now must accommodate "mixed" and permit "mixed" to be ever-so-broadly defined. Even the term "family" is changing, because those who now identify and unify themselves as partners perform many of the functions that the (traditional) two-gender family has performed.

Disability is a natural part of life, and how we embrace it or fail to embrace it reflects our social values and shapes our societal quality of life. So, let us imagine, and more; let us start our embrace of the natural by changing the structure of our education system to match the structure of our country and our families. To do so is to change our schools, but more it is to change society. Educational reform begets societal reform. If our children are to represent the future of our society, the inclusive future we profess to want, how can we be one nation if we teach our children through two separate systems of education, and how can we give a message of "welcome" to those who face impairments if we start by excluding them?

Leaving IDEA and NCLB intact, as they are today, perpetuates the educational divide that we created years ago, with all of the best intentions. We all need support. But we need and benefit most when we get it jointly. Lennon teaches us to imagine. Imagine: we can be one people, one nation, not divided. Swift teaches us to be immodest: We make the not-so-modest proposal of one law. All means all, yes?

"Because she is different, she is often seen as an 'Other,' labeled in ways that negate her full personhood and the complexities of her identity."

The Mother of a Student with Learning Disabilities Calls for More Integrated Learning Environments

Personal Narrative

Leigh M. O'Brien

In the following viewpoint, written in 2006, Leigh M. O'Brien recounts her experiences with her twelve-year-old daughter Lydia, who has developmental and learning disabilities. O'Brien describes the difficulty she and her daughter face in a typical week, showing how the way other people treat her daughter decreases Lydia's motivation to do things, such as go to school or develop relationships with other children. O'Brien contends that if society was to change and become more inclusive and accepting of individuals with disabilities, many of these problems would cease to negatively impact her and her daughter's lives and the lives of those who are in

*similar situations. Leigh M. O'Brien is a teacher-education profes-
sor at State University New York at Geneseo.*

My daughter Lydia, now 12, is a child with "special needs"—
at least in U.S. school settings. The most recent categori-
zation of her for the purposes of her Individualized Education
Plan (IEP) is "cognitive impairment—mild." If forced, I describe
her as having general developmental delays. Thus, in the popular
lexicon, especially with regard to schooling, she is one of "those"
children (as in, "I don't want to work with *those* children.") So
others position her; so she is hailed. I ask here, can she/we resist those positionings? Can she learn to refuse the interpella-
tion? How might school structures and pedagogical approaches
change so that she is not so uncomfortably positioned?

In this paper I want to trouble—in two senses—the identity
that bends Lydia and me over backward, the identity that positions her so painfully. That is, I am troubled by the identity that
is ascribed to her, and I also want to challenge or trouble the
ascription of the identity. Those who are labeled are reduced, as
signifiers become identities; there's always more—they're always
more. Although obviously personal and idiosyncratic, I hope
her/our experiences will resonate with others attempting to deal
with similar positions—both those who share similar identity
positions as well as educators who are working with those in her
position. . . .

I wish to note that I am only addressing one facet of Lydia's
identity here. Identity is multiple, contradictory, and dynamic,
and she, like everyone else, is a multi-faceted being with many
complex overlapping identities. Further, Lydia is not merely a pas-
sive recipient of an ascribed identity. She resists, but is also increasingly complicit in the active construction of her identity as
a child with, as she says, "special learning needs." That she now
so self-identifies speaks to the power of this discourse. However,
self-identifying in this way doesn't mean Lydia has a positive view
of her positioning. As I was preparing to present the first iteration

of this paper, I worried I might be attributing inaccurate feelings to her so I asked her how she felt about being labeled as a child with special needs. She fired back with no hesitation, "I hate it!". . .

The story I tell is both of ours, but for now I am the one telling it. In the near future, as Lydia's awareness and ability to tell her life grows, I want her voice to be heard more clearly. Rather than me speaking and writing *about* her, I hope we will speak and write together. What we can learn about difference by attending to both the child with disabilities and her mother should move us away from the notion that the child is necessarily an "other" to the mother . . . or vice versa. We need to hear *both* voices; they need to hear each other; and each must be believed if "difference" is to make a difference.

A Typical Week

To provide an idea of what our lived lives are like, I will first relate a typical, though constructed, week during the winter of one elementary school year in order to make our intersecting challenges a bit more concrete. I also want to point out that despite the many challenges we face, our lives are no doubt much easier than those without our many privileges of skin color, social class, and language: we are European American, middle class, and English is our first language. In addition, as a former preschool teacher and current professor of education, I have both educational and experiential familiarity with schooling, and hence social capital on which I can and do draw.

Monday mornings are almost always challenging as Lydia does not enjoy school—not surprisingly since it's such a struggle for her—and so often resists going. Further, she is what some call a difficult or high-maintenance child . . . , and persistence/stubbornness is one of her character traits. Thus, we often argue vociferously about whether she is sick or schools will be closed due to snow or about something else that allows Lydia to question the inevitable. Frankly, I understand why she does not enjoy school, and so I have a hard time pushing her to go.

Once I get her on the bus, I do a little exercise and then go to the office where I will stay until 5:30. Some days I get a call that Lydia is not feeling well and is in the nurse's office; most often these are "false alarms" that have much to do with her unhappiness at school but they are unsettling nonetheless. During the afternoon I go to my counselor on campus for some emotional support as I am feeling overwhelmed trying to single handedly arrange for our pending six-month stay in Sweden where I will study Swedish schooling for young children with special needs. Counseling has become a necessity for me at times to help me cope with my multiple responsibilities.

Most evenings we unwind a little before doing homework and attending to other chores. Sometimes we take a walk or go to the library, and frequently Lydia asks if she can call a friend to come over. Wanting her to have at least a few friends, I sometimes feel I must be "super mom." She wants friends to come over to play, to stay for dinner or overnight, to go the amusement park with us. We have kids' parties for every conceivable occasion, and take her friends with us to the library, coffee shop, and local events, but still together suffer the rejection of numerous "no, sorry, not today" responses or unreturned messages.

Long Days Are a Strain

Tuesdays are a long day for me/us as I almost always teach a class until seven P.M. This means that each semester I have to have a sitter who has a car and can pick Lydia up at child care, take her home, feed her dinner, and so forth. This semester we have been fortunate that last semester's sitter is available Tuesday evenings; many semesters I have to find a new sitter who can do all this—and who enjoys being with/can handle Lydia.

Wednesday this week begins with one of my least-favorite activities, a before-school "team meeting" at Lydia's school. At these monthly meetings, the teachers and support staff who work with Lydia share their observations on her academics and behavior. The news is not often good, so I find myself a bit defensive and worried prior to these meetings. . . . The school and I often disagree about what is "best" for Lydia, and it is impossible for me to take off my early childhood teacher educator hat when addressing her education. Lydia must come with me, and this year she has even participated toward the end of each meeting which is interesting and necessary as she ages, but also stressful because of her difficulties in understanding the nature of her disability, and, I believe, the power she rightly perceives the school people having. It's painful for me to watch her struggle to be brave and "grown up" as the school professionals talk about her "needs" and their plans for her education.

Wednesdays are rather long days for us, as I teach a late-night class. This year Lydia has been coming home on the bus Wednesdays and we are together for a couple of hours until I go back to teach until 10 P.M. This semester we went through three sitters (and two nights of Lydia with me in class) until I found someone who could watch her. In addition to the stress of finding competent care, I feel guilty these nights because someone else puts Lydia to bed, and she often compounds my guilt by leaving a sweet message on my office answering machine about how much she loves and really, really, *really* misses me.

Grieving and Feeling Guilty

Lydia has Girl Scouts on many *Thursdays;* today I have to pick her up early from Scouts to take her to the doctor's office to get a prescription for her enuresis [inability to control urination]. Unfortunately, we get to the office a little late, and the doctor will not see us. We reschedule for the following week, meaning more time off work for me and a longer wait to address this problem. Lydia sees several doctors for problems related to her delays. For example, she wears a back brace for scoliosis and we go regularly to both her orthopedist specialist and the prosthetics office to check her progress and the effectiveness of the brace. Sometimes I have to take her out of school, and almost always I have to leave work.

Friday morning I attend a workshop on "dealing with oppositional children." I choose to attend in part for professional insight, but, I must admit, more for help dealing with Lydia who has been more oppositional of late. While I find the workshop very interesting, all of the good doctor's examples are about children with average to above average intelligence. When I tell him about our situation, he admits he doesn't really know what to do with a child who is both developmentally delayed *and* oppositional. Although I find some of the information helpful, I leave feeling more than a bit depressed. Situations like this are reminders that no matter how much I might want it to be so, Lydia will never be able to do what children who are typically developing can do. Grieving is an ongoing experience when you have a child who has disabilities.

I spend *Saturdays and Sundays* trying to get caught up on all the other things I need and want to do that I rarely have time to do during the week. I also spend the weekend feeling guilty that I can't spend more time with Lydia because I am *doing* all these things. Lydia spends the weekend waiting for me to do these things or reluctantly helping me. Mostly her weekend is spent trying to find friends to come over and play or do something outside the home with us. If Lydia has a long weekend off from school, I will take her to meet her dad at a mid-way point and then drive back home for some much-needed rest and relaxation. Although I am happy to have a little time to myself every now and again, I also miss her and worry about her and cannot wait for her to come back so that we are together, our lives whole again.

Defined as an "Other"

In many ways Lydia is *like* others in that she lives a complex life with numerous dimensions. But, because of her ascribed position as a child with disabilities/special needs she is also *different* from others. And because she is different, she is often seen as an "Other," labeled in ways that negate her full personhood and the complexities of her identity. Rather than being herself, subject of her own life, she is defined as the colonized other/object. Being defined in school settings as an Other limits Lydia's ability to construct her own identity. This positioning also causes feelings of shame and pain for Lydia, and pain, loss, and grief for me as her mother. . . .

Lydia and I have felt the pain of those labels, of that kind of separation. While her rights to education have been upheld, perhaps, Lydia has been put into categories based on the current definition of her disability, and then separated out (i.e., grouped with other children with perceived special needs) as often as the school/district/Committee on Special Education (CSE) has been able to get away with it. However, being a believer in inclusion and having a fair amount of social capital in this arena because of my education and job, I have every year insisted that Lydia be placed in a class with her typically developing peers. Despite my efforts, because most of the other children with special needs have been removed ("so their needs can be better met," I have been told more than once) and because, in my opinion, her school doesn't really believe in inclusion, as in the question asked by a parent representative to the CSE, "Wouldn't she be happier in a class where *all* the children are different?" Lydia still stands out because in her class only *she* has to go to Resource Room for "special help." Only *she* needs an aide to help her "do her work/stay on task." Only *she* is identified as "different." She just does not fit in, at least not in our upper-middle-class neighborhood and school where most of the children do very well academically. Her discomfort is, then, not caused by her disability so much as it is caused by active marginalization, isolation, and the lack of existing supports. . . .

Everyone Is Rich in Potential

My daughter and I are tired of being bent over backward by her ascribed labels. As do others in her position, she wants to be known by her name, not her label, and appreciated for her personality, interests, and abilities—that is, who she is. Her disability is only one of many characteristics of her whole persona. She is not her diagnosis or "category." Her potential cannot be defined by her disability label. I want her to have teachers who reflect on and actualize a posture that brings full acceptance to the humanity of her person.

I hope others will join those of us trying to get out of painful positions as we work to construct a new society where each child, each person is seen as being rich in potential; as having power, dignity, and many, varied strengths. Work with us as we fight to move away from a conceptualization of difference as deviance or deficit. Join us as we challenge, and, I hope, dismantle, cultural borders including attitudes toward disability as well as institutional structures that separate and exclude people with disabilities from their peers. Help us resist those who would hail others exclusively or primarily by their socially constructed categories; help children with disabilities reclaim their own identities and their own places in the social formation of schooling. Be our allies as we attempt to re-write the scripts that confine and try to refuse the interpellations that highlight differences while downplaying our commonalities.

> "The [Education for all Handicapped
> Children Act] confers upon disabled
> students an enforceable substantive
> right to public education in
> participating states."

Students with Disabilities Cannot Be Moved from Their Educational Placement Without Proper Evaluation

The Supreme Court's Decision

William J. Brennan

In two separate incidents in 1980, the San Francisco Unified School District (SFUSD) expelled students with disabilities from school after they had violent outbursts stemming from their disabilities. The students filed lawsuits against the school district in protest of their expulsions and called for an Individualized Education Plan (IEP) review process to determine appropriate punishment and school placement. In the following viewpoint, which is the US Supreme Court ruling on Honig v. Doe (1988), Justice William J. Brennan delivers the opinion of the court, finding that in accordance with the Education for All Handicapped Children Act of 1975 (EHA), the schools must allow the students undergoing disciplinary hearings to remain in school until the hearings determine the appropriate

William J. Brennan, Opinion of the court, *Honig v. Doe,* US Supreme Court, January 20, 1988.

course of action. While the school district maintains that this could place administrators, teachers, and other students at risk, Brennan argues that this process ensures that no student is excluded from participation in class and that the punishment is appropriate for the student. Still, the court notes that if a student is an imminent threat to others, schools can suspend the student for ten days until the hearing process is completed. Known for his liberal leanings, William J. Brennan served as a Supreme Court associate justice from 1956 to 1990.

As a condition of federal financial assistance, the Education for all Handicapped Children Act [1975] requires States to ensure a "free appropriate public education" for all disabled children within their jurisdictions. In aid of this goal, the Act establishes a comprehensive system of procedural safeguards designed to ensure parental participation in decisions concerning the education of their disabled children and to provide administrative and judicial review of any decisions with which those parents disagree. Among these safeguards is the so-called "stay-put" provision, which directs that a disabled child "shall remain in [his or her] then current educational placement" pending completion of any review proceedings, unless the parents and state or local educational agencies otherwise agree. Today we must decide whether, in the face of this statutory proscription, state or local school authorities may nevertheless unilaterally exclude disabled children from the classroom for dangerous or disruptive conduct growing out of their disabilities. In addition, we are called upon to decide whether a district court may, in the exercise of its equitable powers, order a State to provide educational services directly to a disabled child when the local agency fails to do so.

A Right to a Free and Appropriate Public Education

In the Education for All Handicapped Children Act, Congress sought "to assure that all handicapped children have available to them . . . a free appropriate public education which emphasizes special education and related services designed to meet their unique needs, [and] to assure that the rights of handicapped children and their parents or guardians are protected." When the law was passed in 1975, Congress had before it ample evidence that such legislative assurances were sorely needed: 21 years after this Court declared education to be "perhaps the most important function of state and local governments," *Brown v. Board of Education* (1954), Congressional studies revealed that better than half of the Nation's eight million disabled children were not receiving appropriate educational services. Indeed, one out of every eight of these children was excluded from the public school system altogether; many others were simply "warehoused" in special classes or were neglectfully shepherded through the system until they were old enough to drop out. Among the most poorly served of disabled students were emotionally disturbed children: Congressional statistics revealed that for the school year immediately preceding passage of the Act, the educational needs of 82 percent of all children with emotional disabilities went unmet.

Although these educational failings resulted in part from funding constraints, Congress recognized that the problem reflected more than a lack of financial resources at the state and local levels. Two federal-court decisions [*Mills v. Board of Education of the District of Columbia* (1972) and *PARC v. Pennsylvania* (1972)], which the Senate Report characterized as "landmark," demonstrated that many disabled children were excluded pursuant to state statutes or local rules and policies, typically without any consultation with, or even notice to, their parents. Indeed, by the time of the EHA's enactment, parents had brought legal challenges to similar exclusionary practices in 27 other states.

In responding to these problems. Congress did not content itself with passage of a simple funding statute. Rather, the EHA confers upon disabled students an enforceable substantive right

No Child Left Behind Act Negatively Impacted Special Education

In January 2002, No Child Left Behind [NCLB] was signed into law. In its quest for reading and math proficiencies, NCLB called for standardized testing to show that schools, classrooms, and teachers were helping students make "adequate yearly progress" towards government-instituted and mandated test scores. In this first rendition, NCLB made no distinction between special ed and regular students. Rather, special ed students were to be tested with everyone else, their scores thrown into the same murky pot as everybody else's, affecting overall school performance marks, funding, and in some states, special education students' opportunities to move from one grade level to the next. As a result, special education curriculums have narrowed. . . .

After much debate about the fairness of requiring the same performance from learning-disabled students as those without disabilities, the Department of Education changed its policy slightly, allowing for up to 1 percent of a state's students to take some sort of "alternative assessment" (despite the fact that 10 percent of students in the United States are classified as special ed). . . . The only difference is that academic-achievement standards and testing methods for special education students are modified; everybody's still expected to know the same things, whether or not these things are actually worth knowing.

Beth Peterson, "Special Ed," Fourth Genre,
vol. 14, no. 1, Spring 2012.

to public education in participating States and conditions federal financial assistance upon a State's compliance with the substantive and procedural goals of the Act. Accordingly, States seeking to qualify for federal funds must develop policies assuring all disabled children the "right to a free appropriate public education," and must file with the Secretary of Education formal plans mapping out in detail the programs, procedures and timetables under which they will effectuate these policies. Such plans must assure that, "to the maximum extent appropriate," States will "mainstream" disabled children, i.e., that they will educate them with children who are not disabled, and that they will segregate or otherwise remove such children from the regular classroom setting "only when the nature or severity of the handicap is such that education in regular classes . . . cannot be achieved satisfactorily."

Individualized Educational Programs Ensure Rights

The primary vehicle for implementing these congressional goals is the "individualized educational program" (IEP), which the EHA mandates for each disabled child. Prepared at meetings between a representative of the local school district, the child's teacher, the parents or guardians, and, whenever appropriate, the disabled child, the IEP sets out the child's present educational performance, establishes annual and short-term objectives for improvements in that performance, and describes the specially designed instruction and services that will enable the child to meet those objectives. The IEP must be reviewed and, where necessary, revised at least once a year in order to ensure that local agencies tailor the statutorily required "free appropriate public education" to each child's unique needs.

Envisioning the IEP as the centerpiece of the statute's education delivery system for disabled children, and aware that schools had all too often denied such children appropriate educations without in any way consulting their parents, Congress repeatedly emphasized throughout the Act the importance and indeed the necessity of parental participation in both the development of the IEP and any subsequent assessments of its effectiveness. Accordingly, the Act establishes various procedural safeguards that guarantee parents both an opportunity for meaningful input into all decisions affecting their child's education and the right to seek review of any decisions they think inappropriate. These safeguards include the right to examine all relevant records pertaining to the identification, evaluation and educational placement of their child; prior written notice whenever the responsible educational agency proposes (or refuses) to change the child's placement or program; an opportunity to present complaints concerning any aspect of the local agency's provision of a free appropriate public education; and an opportunity for "an impartial due process hearing" with respect to any such complaints.

At the conclusion of any such hearing, both the parents and the local educational agency may seek further administrative review and, where that proves unsatisfactory, may file a civil action in any state or federal court. In addition to reviewing the administrative record, courts are empowered to take additional evidence at the request of either party and to "grant such relief as [they] determine is appropriate." The "stay-put" provision at issue in this case governs the placement of a child while these often lengthy review procedures run their course. It directs that:

> During the pendency of any proceedings . . . , unless the State or local educational agency and the parents or guardian otherwise agree, the child shall remain in the then current educational placement of such child. . . .

The present dispute grows out of the efforts of certain officials of the San Francisco Unified School District (SFUSD) to expel two emotionally disturbed children from school indefinitely for violent and disruptive conduct related to their disabilities. . . .

The EHA Mandates That Children "Stay-Put"

The language of [the "stay-put" provision] is unequivocal. It states plainly that during the pendency of any proceedings initiated under the Act, unless the state or local educational agency and the parents or guardian of a disabled child otherwise agree, "the child SHALL remain in the then current educational placement." Faced with this clear directive, petitioner asks us to read a "dangerousness" exception into the stay-put provision on the basis of either of two essentially inconsistent assumptions: first, that Congress thought the residual authority of school officials to exclude dangerous students from the classroom too obvious for comment; or second, that Congress inadvertently failed to provide such authority and this Court must therefore remedy the oversight. Because we cannot accept either premise, we decline petitioner's invitation to re-write the statute.

Petitioner's arguments proceed, he suggests, from a simple, common-sense proposition: Congress could not have intended the stay-put provision to be read literally, for such a construction leads to the clearly unintended, and untenable, result that school districts must return violent or dangerous students to school while the often lengthy EHA proceedings run their course. We think it clear, however, that Congress very much meant to strip schools of the unilateral authority they had traditionally employed to exclude disabled students, particularly emotionally disturbed students, from school. In so doing, Congress did not leave school administrators powerless to deal with dangerous students; it did, however, deny school officials their former right to "self-help," and directed that in the future the removal of disabled students could be accomplished only with the permission of the parents or, as a last resort, the courts.

Court Rulings Are the Basis for EHA

As noted above, Congress passed the EHA after finding that school systems across the country had excluded one out of every eight disabled children from classes. In drafting the law, Congress was largely guided by the recent decisions in *Mills v. Board of Education of the District of Columbia*, (1972), and *PARC [v. Pennsylvania]* (1972), both of which involved the exclusion of hard-to-handle disabled students. *Mills* in particular demonstrated the extent to which schools used disciplinary measures to bar children from the classroom. There, school officials had labeled four of the seven minor plaintiffs "behavioral problems," and had excluded them from classes without providing any alternative education to them or any notice to their parents. After finding that this practice was not limited to the named plaintiffs but affected in one way or another an estimated class of 12,000 to 18,000 disabled students, the District Court enjoined future exclusions, suspensions, or expulsions "on grounds of discipline."

Congress attacked such exclusionary practices in a variety of ways. It required participating States to educate all disabled children, regardless of the severity of their disabilities and included within the definition of "handicapped" those children with serious emotional disturbances. It further provided for meaningful parental participation in all aspects of a child's educational placement, and barred schools, through the stay-put provision, from changing that placement over the parent's objection until all review proceedings were completed. Recognizing that those proceedings might prove long and tedious, the Act's drafters did not intend [the stay-put provision] to operate inflexibly, and they therefore allowed for interim placements where parents and school officials are able to agree on one. Conspicuously absent from [the stay-put provision], however, is any emergency exception for dangerous students. This absence is all the more telling in light of the injunctive decree issued in *PARC*, which permitted school officials unilaterally to remove students in "'extraordinary circumstances.'" Given the lack of any similar exception in *Mills*, and the close attention Congress devoted to these "landmark" decisions, we can only conclude that the omission was intentional; we are therefore not at liberty to engraft onto the statute an exception Congress chose not to create.

Educators Can Discipline Students Appropriately

Our conclusion that [the stay-put provision] means what it says does not leave educators hamstrung. The Department of

Two students work together in a non-separated classroom environment. In Honig v. Doe *(1988), a "stay put" provision mandates that a child cannot be moved from his or her educational placement because of disability-related behavioral problems until thorough review proceedings are completed.* © KidStock/Blend Images/Getty Images.

Education has observed that, "[w]hile the [child's] placement may not be changed [during any complaint proceeding], this does not preclude the agency from using its normal procedures for dealing with children who are endangering themselves or others." Such procedures may include the use of study carrels, time-outs, detention, or the restriction of privileges. More drastically, where a student poses an immediate threat to the safety of others, officials may temporarily suspend him or her for up to 10 school days. This authority, which respondent in no way disputes, not only ensures that school administrators can protect the safety of others by promptly removing the most dangerous of students, it also provides a "cooling down" period during which officials can initiate IEP review and seek to persuade the child's parents to agree to an interim placement. And in those cases in which the parents of a truly dangerous child adamantly refuse to permit any change in placement, the 10-day respite gives school officials an opportunity to invoke the aid of the courts under 1415(e)(2), which empowers courts to grant any appropriate relief.

Petitioner contends, however, that the availability of judicial relief is more illusory than real, because a party seeking review under 1415(e)(2) must exhaust time-consuming administrative remedies, and because under the Court of Appeals' construction of [the stay-put provision], courts are as bound by the stay-put provision's "automatic injunction," as are schools. It is true that judicial review is normally not available under 1415(e)(2) until all administrative proceedings are completed, but as we have previously noted, parents may by-pass the administrative process where exhaustion would be futile or inadequate. While many of the EHA's procedural safeguards protect the rights of parents and children, schools can and do seek redress through the administrative review process, and we have no reason to believe that Congress meant to require schools alone to exhaust in all cases, no matter how exigent the circumstances. The burden in such cases, of course, rests with the school to demonstrate the futility or inadequacy of administrative review, but nothing in 1415(e)(2) suggests that schools are completely barred from attempting to make such a showing. Nor do we think that [the stay-put provision] operates to limit the equitable powers of district courts such that they cannot, in appropriate cases, temporarily enjoin a dangerous disabled child from attending school.

Schools Can Seek Injunctive Relief

As the EHA's legislative history makes clear, one of the evils Congress sought to remedy was the unilateral exclusion of disabled children by SCHOOLS, not courts, and one of the purposes of [the stay-put provision], therefore, was "to prevent SCHOOL officials from removing a child from the regular public school classroom over the parents' objection pending completion of the review proceedings." The stay-put provision in no way purports to limit or pre-empt the authority conferred on courts by 1415(e)(2); indeed, it says nothing whatever about judicial power.

In short, then, we believe that school officials are entitled to seek injunctive relief under 1415(e)(2) in appropriate cases. In any such action, [the stay-put provision] effectively creates a presumption in favor of the child's current educational placement which school officials can overcome only by showing that maintaining the child in his or her current placement is substantially likely to result in injury either to himself or herself, or to others. In the present case, we are satisfied that the District Court, in enjoining the state and local defendants from indefinitely suspending respondent or otherwise unilaterally altering his then current placement, properly balanced respondent's interest in receiving a free appropriate public education in accordance with the procedures and requirements of the EHA against the interests of the state and local school officials in maintaining a safe learning environment for all their students.

| *"To shelter handicapped students from disciplinary sanctions would be to shelter them from the realities of life."*

Schools Must Appropriately Discipline Students with Disabilities Within the Mandated Guidelines

Mitchell L. Yell

In the following viewpoint, special education professor Mitchell L. Yell outlines the common law principles that have been developed through court findings to guide the disciplinary actions educators take to address the misbehavior of children with disabilities. These principles include limits on the amount of time children can be suspended, the procedures that must be followed in suspension and expulsion hearings, and the action schools can take when students become too disruptive to remain in the classroom. While Yell believes that the US Supreme Court decision in Honig v. Doe *in 1988 generally supports the body of common law principles he describes, he worries that the language of the finding leaves some questions unanswered and room for misinterpretation of the ruling. Thus he concludes that in order to ensure that schools have the ability to dis-*

Mitchell L. Yell, "*Honig v. Doe*: The Suspension and Expulsion of Handicapped Students," *Exceptional Children*, vol. 56, no. 1, September 1989, pp. 60–69. Copyright © 1989 by Council for Exceptional Children. All rights reserved. Reproduced by permission.

cipline their students in accordance with the common law principles advanced by the courts, school officials must determine whether the behavior represents a threat to students and school personnel, whether the misbehavior results from the student's disability, and whether the student's educational placement is appropriate. By answering these questions with assistance from the student's parents, Yell maintains that schools will retain the ability to discipline students in a manner that advances both the individual's education and guarantees a positive learning environment for other students.

Public Law 94-142 [or P.L. 94-142, also known as the Education for All Handicapped Children Act of 1975] and regulations implementing the law provide for a free, appropriate public education for handicapped children. However, neither the law nor the regulations address the issue of the discipline of handicapped students. The result has been confusion and uncertainty among special educators and administrators concerning their rights and responsibilities in [this] area.

The courts have been forced into this vacuum, acting as arbiters, having to balance the rights of the handicapped with the school's duty to maintain order and discipline and to provide an appropriate education for all children. A substantial body of litigation has emerged concerning these issues, especially regarding the suspension and expulsion of handicapped students. In interpreting existing laws and regulations, the courts have fashioned a body of common law (law based on court decisions rather than legislatively enacted law) which has helped to clarify this balance. The issue remains unclear, however, because much of this litigation has been contradictory and the decisions by the courts apply only to their particular jurisdiction (e.g., decisions by the 9th Circuit Court apply only to the ninth circuit). On January 20, 1988, the Supreme Court issued a ruling in *Honig v. Doe* that should serve to remove the confusions and uncertainty surrounding these issues. Supreme Court rulings become the law of the land; therefore, this ruling is binding on all schools in the United States. . . .

Common Law Principles

Common law is defined in Barron's Law Dictionary as a system of law "which is based on judicial precedent rather than statutory laws, which are legislative enactments." It is derived from principles based on judicial reasoning and common sense, rather than rules of law. These principles are determined by social needs and have changed in accordance with changes in these needs. The body of common law dealing with the suspension and expulsion of handicapped students has been developed in a number of federal cases. . . .

The common law principles developed from the cases . . . are instructive and can guide the development of school disciplinary policies with handicapped students. These principles retain their significance after *Honig v. Doe* because the Supreme Court's ruling did not address all pertinent issues.

Principle 1. Temporary suspensions are available for use in disciplining handicapped students. Schools have a right and duty to maintain discipline and order. The courts have consistently held that short-term suspensions (of less than 10 days) are neither changes in educational placement nor a cessation of educational services and that these suspensions are therefore available for use with handicapped students. Serial, indefinite, or lengthy suspensions (of more than 10 days), however, are not permitted. In a number of cases in which suspensions of a lengthy nature were used, the courts have considered them to be expulsions. Attempts to obfuscate expulsion by using suspensions in this manner have not been tolerated by the courts.

Principle 2. Expulsions and lengthy suspensions are changes in educational placement which trigger the procedural safeguards of P.L. 94-142. The courts have stated that expelling or suspending a handicapped student for a lengthy period of time (more than 10 days) is tantamount to changing his or her educational placement. According to P.L. 94-142, the educational

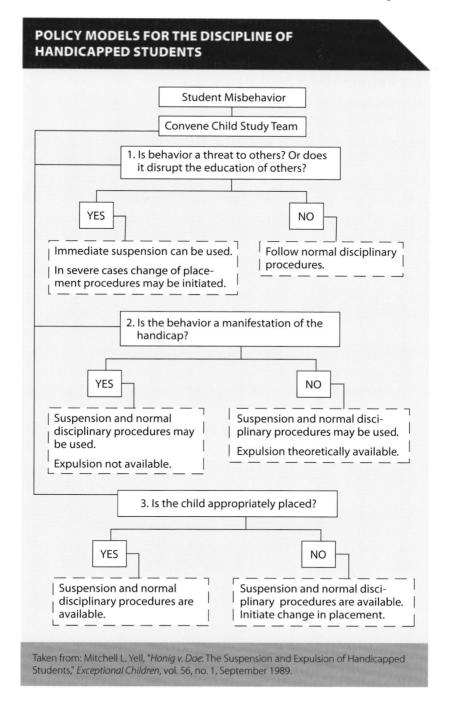

POLICY MODELS FOR THE DISCIPLINE OF
HANDICAPPED STUDENTS

Student Misbehavior

Convene Child Study Team

1. Is behavior a threat to others? Or does it disrupt the education of others?

YES

Immediate suspension can be used.

In severe cases change of placement procedures may be initiated.

NO

Follow normal disciplinary procedures.

2. Is the behavior a manifestation of the handicap?

YES

Suspension and normal disciplinary procedures may be used.

Expulsion not available.

NO

Suspension and normal disciplinary procedures may be used.

Expulsion theoretically available.

3. Is the child appropriately placed?

YES

Suspension and normal disciplinary procedures are available.

NO

Suspension and normal disciplinary procedures are available.

Initiate change in placement.

Taken from: Mitchell L. Yell, "*Honig v. Doe*: The Suspension and Expulsion of Handicapped Students," *Exceptional Children*, vol. 56, no. 1, September 1989.

placement of a handicapped child cannot be changed unless certain procedural safeguards are followed.

The Relationship Between the Handicapping Condition and the Misbehavior

Principle 3. A trained and knowledgeable group of persons must determine whether a causal relationship exists between a child's handicapping conditions and the misbehavior. Only if no relationship exists can a handicapped child be expelled. The courts have recognized that schools have a limited right to suspend and expel handicapped students. Before schools take an action of this nature, however, a trained and knowledgeable group of persons must determine whether a causal relationship exists between the student's handicapping condition and the misbehavior. This group must possess specialized knowledge about the student's handicapping condition. The decision concerning the relationship of the behavior and the handicap must not be a unilateral administrative decision, and cannot be made by persons not knowledgeable about the student's handicap (e.g., a school board).

If a relationship is determined to exist, expulsion is not allowable; however, in the absence of this relationship, expulsion is permitted. Theoretically, expulsion of handicapped students remains available as a disciplinary tool.

In cases in which suspension or expulsion is considered, it is clearly the duty of the schools to convene the Individual Educational Program (IEP) team or the team responsible for determining the appropriate educational setting of the child, and determine whether the child's misbehavior is a manifestation of the child's handicapping condition. The issue of how this determination is to be made is examined in a later section of this article. At present, however, even though the courts have agreed that this is mandatory when considering suspension or expulsion, no judicial guidelines for doing so have been forwarded.

If the team determines that the student's misbehavior and the handicapping condition are not related and the student is expelled, the school district must continue to provide special education services.

Due Process Must Be Followed

Principle 4. Due process procedures are required when suspending or expelling handicapped students. According to the Supreme Court in *Goss v. Lopez* (1975), a student's education is a property right that is protected by the 14th amendment. The court ruled that these rights cannot be taken away for misconduct without adherence to due process procedures. Stating that discipline is essential to the educational process, the court found that behaviors which require immediate and effective disciplinary action may subject the misbehaving student to suspension. The court held that suspension is not only a necessary tool to maintain order and discipline, but also a valuable educational device. Even when students face minimal suspensions of 10 school days or less, however, they *must be* afforded a hearing in which they are presented with the evidence against them, and they must be given an opportunity to present their side of the story. With the exception of an instance in which the student poses a threat to other students or to the educational process, they must be afforded these due process procedures.

Although this case did not involve handicapped students directly, the ruling pertains to them. When imposing suspension or expulsion on handicapped students, school officials will be held to the more extensive due process procedures of P.L. 94-142.

Principle 5. An option open to schools is to transfer a disruptive student to a more restrictive setting. The courts have consistently stated that when a handicapped student is extremely disruptive to the educational process, an option open to the school is to change the student's educational placement by moving him or her to a more restrictive setting. The U.S. Court of

Many have found difficulty in determining how to apply standard models of education, as well as discipline, on those with special needs. © Ableimages/Lifesize/Getty Images.

Appeals, 11th Circuit (*Victoria L. v. District School Board*, 1984), held that not only was the option of transferring a student to a more restrictive placement available, but that it could even be made unilaterally if necessary (e.g., the student's behavior poses a danger to others or impairs the education of other students). When a change in placement is made, the requirements of P.L. 94-142 must be adhered to. . . .

Misbehavior Could Always Be Related to the Handicapping Condition

The decision in *Honig v. Doe* is in agreement with the majority of the past decade of common law that deals with the discipline of handicapped students, with one significant difference. The Supreme Court rejected the "dangerousness exception" to the "stay-put" provision which had been advanced by a number of courts. Although an analysis of the *Honig v. Doe* ruling seems to preclude the use of expulsion with handicapped students, it might be argued that the Supreme Court left the door slightly ajar when it agreed with the appeals court that expulsion of handicapped students for *conduct attributable to their disability* deprives students of their congressionally mandated right to a free appropriate education. This language might be interpreted as the Supreme Court's tacitly agreeing that a handicapped child can be expelled for conduct not attributed to his or her disability.

An analysis of the *Honig v. Doe* decision leads the author to conclude that using expulsion to discipline handicapped students or to exclude a potentially dangerous handicapped student from a classroom is no longer an option available to schools. The Supreme Court, however, quoted the line from *Doe v. Maher* (1986) stating that a handicapped student cannot be expelled for misbehavior that is attributable to the disability. Thus, one might assume that to expel a handicapped child for conduct not attributable to his or her handicapping condition is permissible. This is a tenuous assumption at best. If a school were to adopt this position and expel a handicapped student if the IEP team determined that no relationship existed between the handicap and misbehavior, the school officials would be putting themselves in a legally precarious situation. Given the *Honig v. Doe* decision and existing case law, a good attorney could probably convince a court that misbehavior is always related to the handicapping condition. School districts expelling handicapped students would certainly be inviting administrative reviews and potential litigation (both expensive procedures). Precedence suggests that in such actions school districts would very likely lose, in which case they would open themselves to being sued for attorney's fees. Ignoring the ethical problems inherent in the exclusion of handicapped students from school, the above considerations must lead to the conclusion that the loss of expulsion is really not a great loss. Normal school disciplinary procedure, suspension, and transfer to a more restrictive setting will remain available. . . .

Honig v. Doe Left Many Questions Unanswered

Though the *Honig v. Doe* decision answered a number of important questions concerning the suspension and expulsion of handicapped students, it left a number of questions unanswered. An important question concerns how handicapped students can be disciplined in light of this decision. Despite Justice [William J.] Brennan's assurance that educators will not be "hamstrung" in disciplining handicapped students and that schools may employ normal disciplinary procedures, the matter is far from settled. The first question is: What is a normal disciplinary procedure? What is the status of procedures such as timeout or in-school suspension?

A second unanswered question concerns the court's ruling concerning the interim placement of a handicapped student. According to the court, if a child is a danger to others the school may suspend him or her for up to 10 school days. During this period the school may initiate an IEP review and seek to convince the parents to agree to an interim placement. If the parents refuse the change in placement and the child is "truly dangerous," the school may appeal directly to the courts for relief. The burden of proof would rest on the schools in an appeal of this nature. What would the schools have to prove in such cases?

A third unanswered question concerns the court's ruling that 10-school-day suspensions are allowable. Does this refer to 10 consecutive or 10 cumulative school days? The Office of Civil

Rights stated that suspensions of handicapped students which total more than 10 cumulative days in a school year violate the Rehabilitation Act of 1973. Whether the courts will agree to this interpretation is uncertain. The Supreme Court did not answer these questions; future litigation will probably do so.

Parents and Experts Determine the Best Placement

According to [special education professor Peter E.] Leone, administrators, parents, and teachers must possess the following information to review and monitor disciplinary codes for handicapped children: an understanding of the rights granted to the handicapped children and their parents by P.L. 94-142, an understanding of court decisions involving the discipline of handicapped students, and a series of procedures for guiding their deliberations.

When considering the use of disciplinary procedures with handicapped students, school officials must address the following issues:

1. Is the behavior a threat to the student or others?
2. Is the misbehavior a manifestation of the handicapping condition?
3. Is the handicapped student's current placement appropriate?

These questions must be answered by the student's IEP team (or a similar specialized group of persons), and must not be answered by a school board, principal, or anyone acting unilaterally. The parents must be involved. . . .

The Purpose of Discipline Is to Teach

Because P.L. 94-142 and the regulations implementing it do not address the discipline of handicapped students, the issue has become one of great controversy and confusion. In the absence of statutory law, the courts have fashioned a body of case law. It is important, as the cases illustrate, that special educators and administrators be familiar with the principles of this law to guide them in formulating policies for the discipline of handicapped students. In establishing these policies it is important that the rights of handicapped students are not abridged. Educators should not avoid disciplinary procedures because a student is handicapped. The principles fashioned by the courts place restrictions on actions of the school, but do not prohibit them.

The purpose of discipline is to teach. If students, handicapped and nonhandicapped alike, are to learn their roles and responsibilities in school and society, they must understand the purposes of rules and the consequences of not adhering to those rules. To shelter handicapped students from disciplinary sanctions would be to shelter them from the realities of life.

> *"Section 504 imposes no requirement upon an educational institution to lower or to effect substantial modifications of standards to accommodate a handicapped person."*

A Federally Funded Education Program Can Deny Admittance to a Disabled Individual Based on an Inability to Meet All Program Requirements

The Supreme Court's Decision

Lewis F. Powell

In 1973 Frances Davis applied to the nursing program at Southeastern Community College in North Carolina. The school rejected her application because it determined that Davis would be unable to fulfill all program requirements because she had a hearing disability and had to lip-read in order to understand what others were saying to her. Davis appealed the school's decision on the grounds that it violated Section 504 of the Rehabilitation Act of 1973 and amounted to discrimination based on her handicap. In the following viewpoint, which is the unanimous US Supreme Court ruling in

Lewis F. Powell, Court Opinion, *Southeastern Community College v. Davis*, US Supreme Court, June 11, 1979.

Southeastern Community College v. Davis (1979), Justice Lewis F. Powell finds that colleges that receive federal funds, as Southeastern Community College did, have the right to deny admittance to their programs if an individual is not able to meet all the requirements of the program due to his or her disability. He further maintains that these institutions are not required to make changes to the program to accommodate the individual with a disability if those changes would substantially change the fundamental requisites of the program. Lewis F. Powell served as an associate justice of the Supreme Court from 1972 to 1987.

This is the first case in which this Court has been called upon to interpret Section 504 [of the Rehabilitation Act of 1973]. It is elementary that "[t]he starting point in every case involving construction of a statute is the language itself." Section 504, by its terms, does not compel educational institutions to disregard the disabilities of handicapped individuals or to make substantial modifications in their programs to allow disabled persons to participate. Instead, it requires only that an "otherwise qualified handicapped individual" not be excluded from participation in a federally funded program "solely by reason of his handicap," indicating only that mere possession of a handicap is not a permissible ground for assuming an inability to function in a particular context.

Meeting the Requirements in Spite of a Handicap

The court below, however, believed that the "otherwise qualified" persons protected by Section 504 include those who would be able to meet the requirements of a particular program in every respect except as to limitations imposed by their handicap. Taken literally, this holding would prevent an institution from taking into account any limitation resulting from the handicap, however disabling. It assumes, in effect, that a person need not meet legitimate physical requirements in order to be "otherwise qualified." We think the understanding of the District Court is closer to the plain meaning of the statutory language. An otherwise qualified person is one who is able to meet all of a program's requirements in spite of his handicap.

The regulations promulgated by the Department of HEW [Health, Education, and Welfare] to interpret Section 504 reinforce, rather than contradict, this conclusion. According to these regulations, a "[q]ualified handicapped person" is,

> [w]ith respect to post-secondary and vocational education services, a handicapped person who meets the academic and technical standards requisite to admission or participation in the [school's] education program or activity. . . .

An explanatory note states: "The term 'technical standards' refers to *all* nonacademic admissions criteria that are essential to participation in the program in question."

A further note emphasizes that legitimate physical qualifications may be essential to participation in particular programs. We think it clear, therefore, that HEW interprets the "other" qualifications which a handicapped person may be required to meet as including necessary physical qualifications.

Respondent Calls for the Provision of Auxiliary Aids

The remaining question is whether the physical qualifications Southeastern demanded of respondent might not be necessary for participation in its nursing program. It is not open to dispute that, as Southeastern's Associate Degree Nursing program currently is constituted, the ability to understand speech without reliance on lip-reading is necessary for patient safety during the clinical phase of the program. As the District Court found, this ability also is indispensable for many of the functions that a registered nurse performs.

Respondent contends nevertheless that Section 504, properly interpreted, compels Southeastern to undertake affirmative

The Rehabilitation Act of 1973
Tackles Discrimination

With the passage of the Rehabilitation Act of 1973, the Federal Government undertook a comprehensive program, the effects of which would ultimately open the door to equality for the nation's handicapped. The greatest impact for the handicapped lies within three sections of Title V of the Act: Section 501, mandating non-discrimination by the Federal Government in its own hiring practices; Section 503, prohibiting discrimination and requiring affirmative action on the part of federal contractors who receive more than $2,500 in contracts; and Section 504, which prohibits discrimination against handicapped individuals in any federally funded program or activity. Hence, whereas previous legislation centered on the very limited goal of providing strictly vocational services, Title V of the Rehabilitation Act offered, for the first time, specific civil rights protections by barring the expenditure of federal funds in programs discriminating against the handicapped.

Clyde Mabry Collins Jr., "Retreat of the Rehabilitation Act of 1973: Southeastern Community College v. Davis," Nova Law Journal, vol. 4, 1980.

action that would dispense with the need for effective oral communication. First, it is suggested that respondent can be given individual supervision by faculty members whenever she attends patients directly. Moreover, certain required courses might be dispensed with altogether for respondent. It is not necessary, she argues, that Southeastern train her to undertake all the tasks a registered nurse is licensed to perform. Rather, it is sufficient to make Section 504 applicable if respondent might be able to perform satisfactorily some of the duties of a registered nurse or to hold some of the positions available to a registered nurse.

Respondent finds support for this argument in portions of the HEW regulations discussed above. In particular, a provision applicable to post-secondary educational programs requires covered institutions to make "modifications" in their programs to accommodate handicapped persons, and to provide "auxiliary aids" such as sign language interpreters. Respondent argues that this regulation imposes an obligation to ensure full participation in covered programs by handicapped individuals and, in particular, requires Southeastern to make the kind of adjustments that would be necessary to permit her safe participation in the nursing program.

Fundamental Alteration of a Program Is Not Required

We note first that, on the present record, it appears unlikely respondent could benefit from any affirmative action that the regulation reasonably could be interpreted as requiring. Section 84.44(d)(2), for example, explicitly excludes "devices or services of a personal nature" from the kinds of auxiliary aids a school must provide a handicapped individual. Yet the only evidence in the record indicates that nothing less than close, individual attention by a nursing instructor would be sufficient to ensure patient safety if respondent took part in the clinical phase of the nursing program. Furthermore, it also is reasonably clear that Section 84.44(a) does not encompass the kind of curricular changes that would be necessary to accommodate respondent in the nursing program. In light of respondent's inability to function in clinical courses without close supervision. Southeastern, with prudence, could allow her to take only academic classes. Whatever benefits respondent might realize from such a course of study, she would not receive even a rough equivalent of the training a nursing program normally gives. Such a fundamental alteration in the nature of a program is far more than the "modification" the regulation requires.

Moreover, an interpretation of the regulations that required the extensive modifications necessary to include respondent in the nursing program would raise grave doubts about their validity. If these regulations were to require substantial adjustments in existing programs beyond those necessary to eliminate discrimination against otherwise qualified individuals, they would do more than clarify the meaning of Section 504. Instead, they would constitute an unauthorized extension of the obligations imposed by that statute.

Affirmative Action Is Not a Requisite for Federal Funds

The language and structure of the Rehabilitation Act of 1973 reflect a recognition by Congress of the distinction between the evenhanded treatment of qualified handicapped persons and affirmative efforts to overcome the disabilities caused by handicaps. Section 501(b), governing the employment of handicapped individuals by the Federal Government, requires each federal agency to submit "an affirmative action program plan for the hiring, placement, and advancement of handicapped individuals. . . ." These plans "shall include a description of the extent to which and methods whereby the special needs of handicapped employees are being met." Similarly, Section 503(a), governing hiring by federal contractors, requires employers to "take affirmative action to employ and advance in employment qualified handicapped individuals. . . ." The President is required to promulgate regulations to enforce this section.

Under Section 501(c) of the Act, by contrast, state agencies such as Southeastern are only "encourage[d] . . . to adopt and implement such policies and procedures." Section 504 does not refer at all to affirmative action, and, except as it applies to federal employers, it does not provide for implementation by administrative action. A comparison of these provisions demonstrates that Congress understood accommodation of the needs of handicapped individuals may require affirmative action and knew how to provide for it in those instances where it wished to do so.

US Supreme Court Justice Lewis F. Powell ruled in the 1979 case of Southeastern Community College v. Davis *that state-funded universities have the right to deny admission to those whose disabilities prohibit them from completing some aspect of the work.* © Terry Ashe/Time & Life Pictures/Getty Images.

Although an agency's interpretation of the statute under which it operates is entitled to some deference, "this deference is constrained by our obligation to honor the clear meaning of a statute, as revealed by its language, purpose, and history." *Teamsters v. Daniel*, (1979). Here, neither the language, purpose, nor history of Section 504 reveals an intent to impose an affirmative action obligation on all recipients of federal funds. Accordingly, we hold that, even if HEW has attempted to create such an obligation itself, it lacks the authority to do so.

Educational Programs Are Free to Evaluate Students' Qualifications

We do not suggest that the line between a lawful refusal to extend affirmative action and illegal discrimination against handicapped persons always will be clear. It is possible to envision situations where an insistence on continuing past requirements and practices might arbitrarily deprive genuinely qualified handicapped persons of the opportunity to participate in a covered program. Technological advances can be expected to enhance opportunities to rehabilitate the handicapped or otherwise to qualify them for some useful employment. Such advances also may enable attainment of these goals without imposing undue financial and administrative burdens upon a State. Thus, situations may arise where a refusal to modify an existing program might become unreasonable and discriminatory. Identification of those instances where a refusal to accommodate the needs of a disabled person amounts to discrimination against the handicapped continues to be an important responsibility of HEW.

In this case, however, it is clear that Southeastern's unwillingness to make major adjustments in its nursing program does not constitute such discrimination. The uncontroverted testimony of several members of Southeastern's staff and faculty established that the purpose of its program was to train persons who could serve the nursing profession in all customary ways. This type of purpose, far from reflecting any animus against handicapped individuals is, shared by many, if not most, of the institutions that train persons to render professional service. It is undisputed that respondent could not participate in Southeastern's nursing program unless the standards were substantially lowered. Section 504 imposes no requirement upon an educational institution to lower or to effect substantial modifications of standards to accommodate a handicapped person.

One may admire respondent's desire and determination to overcome her handicap, and there well may be various other types of service for which she can qualify. In this case, however, we hold that there was no violation of Section 504 when Southeastern concluded that respondent did not qualify for admission to its program. Nothing in the language or history of Section 504 reflects an intention to limit the freedom of an educational institution to require reasonable physical qualifications for admission to a clinical training program. Nor has there been any showing in this case that any action short of a substantial change in Southeastern's program would render unreasonable the qualifications it imposed.

> "[The Americans with Disabilities
> Act] eliminate[s] . . . barriers in
> employment, transportation, public
> accommodations, public services,
> and telecommunications."

The Americans with Disabilities Act Will Advance Civil Rights for Disabled Americans

Dick Thornburgh

On July 26, 1990, President George H.W. Bush signed the Americans with Disabilities Act (ADA) into law. The act extends a range of civil rights to individuals with disabilities and prohibits discrimination based on disability. In the following viewpoint, written just months after the ADA became law, US attorney general Dick Thornburgh argues that the ADA will overcome the failures of previous disability rights legislation and ensure accessibility in all aspects of life to individuals with disabilities. He also emphasizes that physical accessibility must be accompanied by a shift in attitude regarding the abilities of individuals who have disabilities. Americans must accept people with disabilities to create a fully inclusive society. According to Thornburgh, the ADA is a first step in bringing about this change. Dick Thornburgh served as US attorney general from 1988 to 1991.

Dick Thornburgh, "The Americans with Disabilities Act: What It Means to All Americans," *Labor Law Journal,* vol. 14, no. 12, December 1990, pp. 803–807. Copyright © 1990 by The Labor Law Journal. All rights reserved. Reproduced by permission.

I t has now been almost three decades since the Civil Rights Act of 1964 first became law. Many of us who participated in those heady, often dangerous, days within [the civil rights] movement can well remember how men and women of good will from all racial, religious, and ethnic strains united and fought valiantly to overcome the systematic denial of the blessings of freedom in our American society.

We all remain dedicated to that goal. But there is an inevitable tendency toward differing views, even toward rising dispute and sometimes faction, the more distant we are from those early days when basic advances were made. No great awakening ever kept everybody "up" forever. We have had more than our share of such dispute over civil rights legislation this year [1990], largely because the present bill [the Civil Rights Act of 1990, which never became law] is embroiled in good faith conflict over what many regard as fine distinctions or "legal technicalities."

I don't shun these legal arguments. I would be happy to discourse on "disparate treatment" of an individual, which we all agree the law should fully remedy, as opposed to "disparate impact" upon a group, which by all past legal principle must first be proved to the court before any remedy is ordered. Just as the former can lead to injustice, the latter can lead to quotas. But as convinced as I am on those points, I see them as secondary to the next great leap forward in the civil rights movement that Congress enacted and President [George H.W.] Bush signed into law this summer: the Americans with Disabilities Act [ADA].

The ADA Extends the Rights of Millions

The impact of ADA is not disparate, but broadening, inclusive and—if you will—re-awakening. Do not let this bright moment in modern American history escape you. Its coming impact upon our communal life can be described in straightforward but startling terms.

On July 26, 1990, President George H.W. Bush signed into law the Americans with Disabilities Act, which granted disabled people a wide range of rights and equal protection. © Barry Thumma/AP Images/Corbis.

Consider these demographic figures. Over thirty million Black Americans make up 12.3 percent of our populace. Other minorities—just over eight million—comprise another 3.4 percent. That total is a full 15.7 percent of our entire population. But 43 million Americans with disabilities represent 17 percent of the nation. We have just seen those who are empowered by our civil rights laws in this country doubled. And though I take these figures from the *rolls* of potential beneficiaries under ADA, I definitely mean it when I say that *rights* are what have truly doubled.

Because each time civil rights are enlarged in this country, they extend over the whole of our society. *All* Americans, not just minorities, are involved in every new extension of such rights. The passage of ADA is truly another emancipation, not only for the 43 million Americans with disabilities who will directly benefit but even more so for the rest of us, now free to benefit from the contributions that these Americans will make to our economy, our communities, and our individual well-being. . . .

The Doors Must Be Widened

A first priority, always, has been to guarantee physical access for the disabled. We are gathered right now in the Ormandy Ball Room of the Hershey Hotel. As opposed to many fine old structures here in Philadelphia from the colonial period on, it was built in 1983 to meet certain needs of those with disabilities. So, without obstruction or hindrance, they have been able to join in today's proceedings. Not even Independence Hall, under retrofit since 1976, is yet that welcoming. Those among us with disabilities can even stay at this hotel, should they wish, in ten bedrooms specially fitted for their use. A ramp from the lobby to the lounge and doors built wide enough to accommodate any of us using a wheelchair send a further positive message of welcome and inclusion.

In a sense, that is what our concern for those with disabilities is all about: widening the doors—a civil right became an architectural imperative. But not just physical doors: also the doors of opportunity for those with disabilities and, among the broader public community, the doors of perception, so that we all recognize the right of people with disabilities to come in to mainstream society; to come in to the restaurant or the Academy of Music or to houses of worship or movie theaters, or aboard the SEPTA bus; to come in, most particularly, to the workplace, and, above all, to long-term prospects for a future life of hope and achievement.

This final widening of the doors through ADA comes after a long legal campaign. The Rehabilitation Act of 1973 was the first milestone, showing that doors could be physically widened and other public access offered, but more important, show-ing that federal employment policy could accommodate those with handicaps. Then came the Education for All Handicapped Children Act [EHA] two years later, which gave a new genera-tion its great opportunity.

The ADA Overcomes Past Failures

[The EHA] set about teaching people with disabilities within the nation's mainstream school systems, guaranteeing an ap-propriate educational placement in the least restrictive setting. In the ensuing fifteen years, an unsighted person or somebody with impaired hearing or mental retardation or using a wheel-chair could learn right alongside others. He or she could have started somewhere between kindergarten through 12th grade and by now be all the way through college. This new genera-tion overcame both their disabilities and the prejudices—often very sympathetic prejudices, the hardest to counter—that their disabilities aroused. They have achieved a high school educa-tion either by diploma or certificate of completion. Many have gone on to college and even advanced degrees. And yearly they are coming into the labor market—150,000 strong. They are well educated, well motivated, well along in understanding what prospects life can really hold for them, and well up on the rights they are determined to secure for themselves under our Constitution.

They are the first generation of Americans with disabilities who will be, in every best sense, fully empowered in the 1990s. And they have now been guaranteed their civil rights under the Americans with Disabilities Act. To touch all its bases, ADA overcomes our past failure to eliminate attitudinal, architectural, and communications barriers in employment, transportation, public accommodations, public services, and telecommunica-tions. In short, it widens all the doors I have spoken of, mandat-ing true access for Americans with disabilities to mainstream society.

The ADA Limits Job Discrimination

First and foremost, the ADA acts against job discrimination in the private sector. At present, 58 percent of all men with disabilities, and 80 percent of all women, are jobless. So long as unemployment continues to be the lifelong fate of two-thirds of those with disabilities, we cannot break the bind of national expenditure for dependence: at least $169 billion annually, some even estimate as high as $300 billion, approaching nearly four percent of the GNP [gross national product].

The ADA legally requires, following Section 504 of the 1973 Rehabilitation Act, that the private employer make reasonable accommodation to the known mental or physical impairments of qualified disabled persons, so long as making that accommodation does not result in an undue hardship on the operations of the employer. This, of course, inevitably raises the question of cost.

But, if this new generation is all that it appears to be, any hardship may well be offset by corresponding gains. Gains in education and brain power and stick-to-itivity which could easily reduce the expense of putting in a ramp or assisting an unsighted or hearing-impaired employee with telecommunication equipment—especially with computer and other technological advances in compensatory assistance.

The President's Committee on Employment of People with Disabilities has already done excellent work to show how any business—from one to 1,000 employees—can economically employ those who are "ready, willing, and available." As Attorney General, I have a role to play, under ADA, in offering technical assistance to any employer, large or small, who is ready to hire from this pool of people with disabilities. It seems highly unlikely that any employer—in a stressed labor market, skewed demographically toward the previously unemployable—is going to undervalue any group's potential contribution. A mind, whatever its limitations or the disability of the body, is still a terrible thing to waste.

Improved Physical Access

The other great widening, under ADA, is in access to general accommodations and public transportation. None of our citizens should have to face preventable obstacles and inconveniences when they go out shopping or to the movies. What is only a curb to most of us may seem like a rugged cliff to somebody using a wheelchair. Not long ago, we saw a man with quadriplegia actually scale El Capitan in the Yosemites. Few of us with two sound arms and two sound legs could manage that feat. So surely, we are ready to help some others conquer these slighter elevations.

ADA keeps the removal of physical barriers reasonably limited to what is "readily achievable," such as are being accomplished at Independence Hall. Its forward-looking emphasis is on new construction, which should at most add one percent to construction costs. Elevators are always the rising exception. The ADA prudently requires that elevators be built in all new construction over three stories, but otherwise only in multilevel shopping malls and other three-story-and-under professional buildings designated by the Office of the Attorney General.

ADA also ends barriers that people with hearing impairments face in using the telephone through auxiliary aids such as nonvoice terminal devices. But auxiliary aids must not, ADA further states, cause an "undue burden." A restaurant should not, for example, have to provide menus in Braille to blind patrons, if the waiter is willing to read the menu—especially at a French restaurant.

Accessible Public Transportation

It is in public transportation that ADA requires a giant step toward physical access within the near-term future—that urban bus systems really kneel down, if you will. All newly built buses must be accessible to persons with disabilities. The ADA does not mandate retrofitting buses already in service. But 35 percent of present urban buses are already accessible and,

Findings and Purpose of the ADA

The Congress finds that

    (1) some 43,000,000 Americans have one or more physical or mental disabilities, and this number is increasing as the population as a whole is growing older;

    (2) historically, society has tended to isolate and segregate individuals with disabilities, and, despite some improvements, such forms of discrimination against individuals with disabilities continue to be a serious and pervasive social problem;

    (3) discrimination against individuals with disabilities persists in such critical areas as employment, housing, public accommodations, education, transportation, communication, recreation, institutionalization, health services, voting, and access to public services;

    (4) unlike individuals who have experienced discrimination on the basis of race, color, sex, national origin, religion, or age, individuals who have experienced discrimination on the basis of disability have often had no legal recourse to redress such discrimination; . . .

It is the purpose of this chapter

    (1) to provide a clear and comprehensive national mandate for the elimination of discrimination against individuals with disabilities;

    (2) to provide clear, strong, consistent, enforceable standards addressing discrimination against individuals with disabilities;

    (3) to ensure that the Federal Government plays a central role in enforcing the standards established in this chapter on behalf of individuals with disabilities; and

    (4) to invoke the sweep of congressional authority . . . in order to address the major areas of discrimination faced day-to-day by people with disabilities.

Americans with Disabilities Act of 1990,
Pub. L. No. 101–336 § 12101 (1991).

for once, the potholes are on our side! Twelve years rattling around our city streets—and especially in Philadelphia—is a long life for any old bus. Attrition and replacement will quickly bring total accessibility to the nation's inner city bus systems. Meanwhile, to make up for any lack of urban transportation for the disabled, the ADA mandates supplementary paratransit services—which 75 percent of urban transit agencies happen to provide already.

Other public transportation systems—AMTRAK, subways, rapid and light rail—are given up to twenty, sometimes thirty years to comply, but we can abide this delay because other ADA provisions largely accommodate the lifestyles of persons with disabilities. We should always be sensitive to the day-to-day living patterns of people with disabilities, and not treat either their rights or their lives in the abstract. What we should notice is that the most important ADA provisions are all of a piece, meeting the actual needs of a populace that lives in a particular, habituated, interactive way.

For example, a major focus of the ADA is against job discrimination. Only, where are the jobs? Increasingly, they are outside the city. But where have persons with disabilities largely chosen to live? Within the city. Why? Because that is where accessible apartments and condos are available in buildings already provided with elevators—including Braille buttons on the operating panels—in neighborhoods where the shops are already retrofitted with ramps. Then how do persons with disabilities get to their place of work, once they gain employment? Only via accessible public urban transport.

Suddenly the right to a seat on the bus—an old, first cause of civil rights protests—is once again vital to the right of employment. Once, the civil rights struggle was not to be forced to sit in the back of the bus on the way to work. Now the struggle is to get on the bus, period, on the way to work. The ADA becomes, in this respect, the enabling act for this new generation of Americans with disabilities, and all those who come after.

Attitudes Must Change, Too

We have seen this intertwining of jobs, public accommodation, and accessible transportation work out right in the nation's capital. In Washington, the traffic pattern followed by persons with disabilities happens to run both ways, particularly on the D.C. Metro. Some travel out of the city as private employees to jobs beyond the Beltway, others come into the central nexus of the U.S. Government as federal employees. But please remember, persons with disabilities originally had to bring suit to gain this access to the Metro.

Now they are accepted as travelling companions on the Metro. What has changed—but must change even more—are attitudes. I have seen this happen as a father emotionally and intimately involved in the life and future of a son who has a disability and as a staunch advocate of civil rights for the disabled. "Ten years ago, you were a patient," says a friend of my wife, from this new generation. "Now you're a client. Formerly, they healed the body and just left you. Now there is so much more understanding and long-term help." The ADA enacts certain accommodations for disabled Americans within the daily, social fabric to help ensure that understanding and long-term help. At the same time, it wisely tempers its punitive measures against those who—whether insensitively or inadvertently—traduce the rights of the disabled. It is social legislation to end barriers, not an instrumentality for continuous and acrimonious litigation.

Still, we do need some consciousness-raising about Americans with disabilities, especially since our mistaken attitudes are often so well-meaning and so ingrained. Every Christmas, for example, we all go through one viewing or another of [British author Charles] Dickens' beloved *A Christmas Carol*. When the tale begins to touch on the fate of Tiny Tim, I often think, frankly, of the need for a rewrite of that classic. In these [19]90s, the first thing we should do is stop calling him Tiny. He ought to be Tim, for the rest of his life. And while it is good of Ebenezer Scrooge to take up Tim's case and try to see that he is cured and throws away his crutch, suppose that Tim doesn't and physically never can? Then what Tim needs is school—as much education as he can absorb, and he should be allowed to keep his crutch beside his desk in the classroom. In fact, if Scrooge really wants to help, he might very well, as a small businessman with less than 15 employees (minus now even Marley), think hard about hiring young Timothy Cratchit after he graduates. And when Tim comes to work, maybe via a kneeling bus, and up a ramp at curbside, Scrooge should see that he can easily access that very high stool where Bob Cratchit once sat before him. That is how we keep that sorry vision of Tim's crutch left to stand forlornly in the fireplace corner from ever happening. What's it doing there, Tim? Bring it to work!

And so to work we must go, to translate the words of the Americans with Disabilities Act into action, into new rights for 43 million American citizens, into lives of dignity, opportunity and achievement for those previously held back from full participation in mainstream America. Let us be on with it!

> *"My dream for the future is that malls and other major points of interest will have some central place where people who need [personal assistance services] can get help."*

A Young Adult Examines the Impact of Personal Assistance Services on Her Life

Personal Narrative

Sascha Bittner

In the following viewpoint, written in 1992, eighteen-year-old Sascha Bittner describes what it is like to have a disability and to need personal assistance services (PAS), or help with the basic tasks of daily living, such as going to the bathroom. Bittner details the frustration she faces when she is in public and cannot get help. She also describes how she was excluded from extracurricular activities at school because of a lack of PAS and accessibility to venues. While Bittner is grateful for the help of her parents, she looks forward to increasing her independence by finding PAS outside the home. Today Sascha Bittner is a disability rights activist who has worked with numerous disability rights groups and served as the chair of the California State Council on Developmental Disabilities.

Sascha Bittner, "PAS from a Teenage Perspective," Personal Perspectives, *World Institute on Disability,* 1992, pp. 31–35.

As an 18-year-old woman with a disability living at home [in San Francisco, California], I have largely relied on my parents or school personnel for personal assistance services [PAS]; my mom actually gets paid by the state of California to be my In-Home Supportive Services provider. As a result of my disability, cerebral palsy, I am quadriplegic, with speech (articulation) and vision impairments. I need personal assistance for many of the routine tasks of daily living, like getting out of bed, getting dressed, going to the bathroom, menstrual care, grooming, bathing, and meal preparation.

One of the major problems of having family members as attendants is that even when we are really upset with each other, my mom or dad still has to take me to the bathroom! It also makes it much harder for all of us to see me as an independent adult when I must depend on them for all my PAS. There are a lot of issues that already come up between teenagers and their parents that become even more complicated by this kind of dependence.

On the positive side, my parents will really go that extra mile for me and do things on very short notice that might be difficult to get other attendants to do. They will do things without regard for the hours or the wages involved. Of course, the solution to this dilemma isn't that people with disabilities should have their parents for personal assistants, but that hours and wages should be adequate for our needs.

Personal Assistance Services Can Be Difficult to Find

The overriding problem I have in terms of being independent in the community is the need for assistance in the bathroom. This simple fact of nature puts a huge constraint on everything I do. I don't need an attendant to hang around with me while I travel on public transportation, go to school, go to the library, go out to eat, etc., etc. But, every few hours I do need someone to take me to the bathroom. If I'm in Berkeley, [California,] I can use the emergency personal assistance services through Vantastic (at seven bucks a pee!), but often I just have to hold it until I get home, or make some arrangement to meet one of my parents. (I might take paratransit or public transportation to meet my parents at work, or one of them might go to where I am.) At other times, I might persuade or pay a friend or acquaintance to help me; however, while I can bear some weight, it is difficult for people not familiar with my particular needs to understand exactly what needs to be done; it becomes a lot easier with a little experience. If I really am desperate (and feeling pretty bold) I might even ask a stranger to help me. This requires very good judgment, because I certainly don't want to get into any kind of unsafe situation. A couple of times when nature has called in a very insistent way during my visits to a local mall, I've asked women at the information desk to help me; it makes it a lot easier when two people can do it, anyway, and I don't think I could have gotten a much safer situation with strangers.

My dream for the future is that malls and other major points of interest will have some central place where people who need PAS can get help. It is stupid to have to hire a personal assistant for an hour or more when you just need one for five minutes in the bathroom! Independent Living Centers might be another good place for such drop-in services, especially if the centers are centrally located. I actually asked for bathroom assistance once at the Berkeley CIL [Center for Independent Living] during another desperate moment; while they agreed to help me that one time, I was politely warned not to try it again.

Lack of PAS at School

PAS was also an important consideration during my elementary and secondary years. Obviously, my parents attended to my needs at home, but I sometimes had trouble getting what I needed at school. In high school, the female para-professional who usually took me to the bathroom only worked until about two hours before school got out. If I wanted to stay after school for a club meeting, or maybe even just really needed to go to the bathroom again (disabled students were heavily discouraged from using the bathroom more than once a day), I just had to manage on my own. If the para was out sick, usually there was a para available from one other class, but sometimes I ended up having to recruit female teachers and even other female students.

Extracurricular activities, unfortunately, were the most problematic in terms of PAS. During the sixth grade, most of my class (this was my first year being fully "mainstreamed") went on a three-day camping trip to a park about 60 miles from where I live in San Francisco. Since only two adults would be supervising an unruly pack of sixth-graders—and one of those adults would only be there for a while—I couldn't attend unless I brought a personal assistant with me. Naturally, that meant my parents ended up accompanying me. While they tried to leave me on my own as much as possible, it was kind of a drag to be the only kid whose parents had to be there. Not to mention that my parents were forced to take off work in order to make this possible for me.

All through my public school years we had to deal with the issue of extracurricular activities. When my classes would go on field trips, my mom would have to provide the transportation and the PAS or I couldn't go. (At that time, the public transportation in San Francisco was not as accessible as it is now, and I had not made it off the waiting list of the paratransit program.) I was in the choir in the seventh and eighth grades, and we went on frequent field trips to attend musical performances or to perform ourselves, and it involved a real commitment by my mom to make sure I could participate.

Also, for any non-school activities like camps, summer programs, and after school programs, PAS was always an issue and usually meant that I would only have the opportunity to attend segregated programs for disabled kids. (The kind of programs offered were rarely ones I was interested in.) A non-segregated social life was virtually impossible, because I wasn't allowed to be part of those kinds of programs. When I did manage to get together socially with non-disabled kids, personal assistance issues again presented limits—for example, if I spent the night at someone else's house, who would provide those services? Usually, kids would have to come over to my house, which meant I didn't get out of the house as much as I would have liked and my parents never got a break.

Schools Have Begun to Make More Activities Accessible

When I was a senior in high school, I actually ended up suing the school district over the inaccessibility of extracurricular activities and the lack of personal assistance services. In the fall of my senior year in high school, an advisory from the Legal Department of the California Department of Education had been sent to all school districts in the state, letting them know they were required by law to hold all school-related activities, including proms, field trips, etc., at accessible sites, with appropriate personal assistance services. If transportation was provided for any students, accessible transportation needed to be provided to disabled students at no extra cost. By this time, I had been to one prom held at an inaccessible site, and to numerous other activities at which no PAS had ever been available (I would have to call my parents to come assist me if the need arose). During the spring semester, a two-day trip to Disneyland, sponsored by the senior class, was planned, along with a senior picnic. Naturally, none of the transportation was accessible, and there were no plans to provide personal assistance services. It was just assumed that my parent should fill in. This time, however, we were more familiar with the law, and decided to file suit through the Disability Rights Education and Defense Fund. The day after the suit was filed, the school district attorney called our attorney to say the district would comply with the law. Part of the agreement to drop the suit was that this policy will be made very clear to all principals, parents and students, so that no other kids would have to go through what my parents and I went through.

Not Everything Can Be Made Accessible

Last spring I was the grand prize winner in an annual essay contest sponsored by the English Speaking Union [ESU] of San Francisco. The prize was a trip to Oxford, England, to attend a summer program at one of the colleges at Oxford University. Normally, the high school senior who wins the contest is given a plane ticket to England and stays in Oxford with an ESU family. Obviously, PAS and wheelchair access issues would mean that I would not be able to follow the usual pattern. To start with, the college that I would be attending was not accessible, and housing was not accessible. More critical even than that, though, was the issue of personal assistance. So the ESU granted me an alternative prize—a trip to England with my parents. We had a really wonderful time, and ended up going to Belgium, France, the Netherlands, Germany, Austria, and Italy, too. My poor parents even got me up to see the completely inaccessible "secret attic" of Anne Frank, and my dad carried my wheelchair up endless flights of stairs (in the Metro in Paris, for example), since there was virtually no accessible public transportation in the cities we visited, and accessible (cheap) lodging was also in short supply. I ended up seeing a lot more of what I wanted to see than if I had been with someone besides my parents, but in the future I want to have other options.

A Transition to More Independence

Next year, for financial reasons, I will be commuting to school at UC [University of California] Berkeley, and my parents will still be providing most of my personal assistance. However, the following year I will live on campus, and participate in the Disabled Students' Resident Program. This will mean a huge change for my family, one that is a little scary but also very exciting. The program at Berkeley will provide me with the assistance and training I need to learn how to function independently in the community and to hire and manage my own personal assistants.

A lot of pressure will be taken off the relationship I have with my parents, but I'm sure it will be hard for all of us to let go, too. I'll also have to adjust to other people doing those intimate things that have largely been left to my family. Still, this transition is what becoming an adult is all about, and I'm looking forward to both the challenges and the new sense of freedom.

> *"As I have evolved as an individual with a disability, so has the [Americans with Disabilities Act]."*

A Man Disabled as a Child Reflects on the Importance of the Americans with Disabilities Act on His Life

Personal Narrative

Adrian Villalobos

Adrian Villalobos was hit by a car when he was eight years old. He suffered injuries that put him in a wheelchair for the rest of his life. In the following viewpoint, Villalobos describes his life after the accident and his experiences with the effects of the recently enacted Americans with Disabilities Act (ADA). He notes the differences between elementary school, where the school was virtually inaccessible and the staff was resistant to help, and middle and high school, where teachers and school administrators actively worked to include him and to make school facilities and activities accessible for him. Villalobos also recounts his experiences in college where accessibility was not a problem, but exclusion still made

Adrian Villalobos, "Testimony of Adrian Villalobos, Intern, National Disability Rights Network, for the House Judiciary Committee Hearing," July 22, 2010.

adapting to a new environment difficult. Villalobos concludes that overall, the ADA made significant, positive impacts on his life and the lives of others with disabilities, but he urges advocates and lawmakers to continue to strive to achieve even greater levels of inclusion.

My name is Adrian Villalobos, and I'm from El Paso, Texas. I am currently [in 2010] an intern at the National Disability Rights Network, through a fellowship from the Southern Education Foundation. I am here in Washington, D.C. to focus on special education policy and accommodations for schoolchildren with disabilities, which is a very pertinent issue to my life.

July is a very significant month for me. I was born in July, and so was the Americans with Disabilities Act [ADA]. I also had a life-changing accident in July. The ADA was three years old when my life changed and I was essentially re-born. Growing up with the ADA, I consider it my metaphorical big brother. On July 9th, 1993, the day after our eighth birthday, my twin and I were playing baseball on the sidewalk in my hometown. I threw him a hardball, and he missed, sending the ball into traffic. Wanting to show off, I darted after the ball into a busy four-lane road. I made it across three lanes safely before being struck and thrown twenty-five feet.

Feeling Rejected

I was in the hospital for two months, and missed my entire summer vacation. The following intensive outpatient rehabilitation cut into the school year and I missed six weeks of classes. It was my first taste of social isolation. When I finally returned to school and the third grade, I was in a wheelchair at an elementary school that was not accessible. The right of people with disabilities to be fully included in society was a new concept, and my parents were unaware of the services I was now entitled to. They met with the school to discuss my return, and one by one the third grade teachers refused to have me in their classrooms.

The intense feeling of rejection my parents experienced on my behalf fueled them to push forward.

Finally a teacher agreed to have me in her classroom. But I couldn't physically get into the school building. The only existing ramps were to some portable classrooms that had been set up at the back of the school to respond to growing school enrolment. With the insistence of my parents, and the ADA gaining momentum, the school moved all the third grade classes into the portables so I could attend school and be with my peers.

My teacher and my twin had to drag my chair through the pebbled walkway all the way around the building to get to the portables and back every day. I was still unable to get into the main school building and none of the restrooms were accessible. To get to the cafeteria and auditorium, which were detached from the main building, I had to enter through a loading dock. I remember my return to school very fondly because of the mutual excitement my peers and I had to see each other once again. They were happy to see me, their friend Adrian, not the kid that came back in a wheelchair.

The ADA Enabled Accessibility

The following school year my class, now fourth grade, was again assigned to the portables. And I still had no access to most of the school building. My parents were frustrated that my school was still inaccessible, and continued to push the principal and school administration. Only this time, a year after the accident, my family was more educated about my rights and pointed to the ADA. The school administration acted.

Ramps to the school building and the cafeteria were built. A bathroom was made accessible. And I was allowed to use the elevator, previously restricted to the custodial staff. This finally gave me access to the nurse's station, located on the second floor. My parents struggled with the school's resistance to creating the most basic accommodations for me. But once they were in place, I felt like I could do what all the other kids could do, and

Adrian Villalobos (right) shakes House Majority Leader Steny Hoyer's hand during a July 2010 hearing on the twentieth anniversary of the Americans with Disabilities Act. © Douglas Graham/Roll Call/Getty Images.

it made me happy. In elementary school, I got a taste of basic accommodations.

The administration at my middle school had a completely different tone. They did not have accessible facilities either, but made major changes to their school to make my experience a positive one. As I was growing, the ADA was growing, and the attitude of inclusion was evolving in a positive way. Physical accommodations were made, not only to the school building, but also to other school facilities. For example, the football field was located on the other side of a busy street—the same busy street where I'd had my accident. Accommodations were made so I wouldn't have to cross that street to cheer on my school's team.

My principal wanted me to have the option to attend any school event or activity I wanted to. He insisted on a modified cello so I could learn the instrument and play in the school orchestra. A lift was built so I could get onto the stage and participate in the drama club. My principal also created a computer club—I was interested in computers. Middle school taught me inclusion.

By high school I had good friends, knew how to navigate El Paso comfortably, and felt self-empowered. I attended high school in a brand new building that was completely accessible. It was 1999, and the ADA was in full swing. Through the National Spinal Cord Association I had the opportunity to see [well-known actor, activist, and quadriplegic] Christopher Reeve speak, and his message about human potential resonated with me. I really understood that perceived limitations are not actual limitations, and that despite my disability, I was responsible for reaching my potential.

Accessible Is Not Equal

With that self-confidence and motivation, I enrolled in a liberal arts college in Ohio. Excited to start something challenging and new, I quickly learned that accessible is not equal. Upon reflection, I could have arrived at this same conclusion in elementary school if I'd been educated about my rights at that young age. The college disability office, with only one staff member, granted me an accessible room with an accessible bathroom and shower. I got a great room and was impressed with the facility when I arrived. The problem with my room was that it was in the lobby of my dorm. Everyone else lived on the other side of locked hallways, in the typical freshman hall setting. I was the guy who lived in the lobby. Socializing is a major pillar of college, and most people meet their friends in their freshman dorms. But I was on the wrong side of those locked doors and freshman halls. The gratitude I'd felt for having an accessible shower quickly turned to a feeling of isolation.

As I evolved and my needs changed, accommodation was no longer adequate. I needed inclusion. The ADA recognized that, too. I didn't survive that college in Ohio. Instead, I transferred to University of Texas, El Paso, back to my friends and family and my network. I moved back into my home, the most accommodating place on earth. Under those circumstances, I did well in college. But even at the University of Texas, El Paso, where I was accommodated and included, there were obstacles to overcome. On my graduation day, for example, I was excluded from the commencement procession because, in the words of university staff, I was a fire hazard.

The Continued Evolution of the ADA Will Advance Inclusion

As I have evolved as an individual with a disability, so has the ADA. The concept of disability rights is no longer new or foreign. Many people and institutions, such as my middle school, have moved beyond the letter of the law and truly embraced its intent. For others, there are still miles to go before they reach real inclusion for individuals with disabilities. I have experienced both. I know how great inclusion is. More importantly, the people in my life have become aware of disability rights.

When I got to [Washington,] DC this summer, a friend who lives here was excited to take me sightseeing. He wondered aloud if certain sights and attractions were wheelchair accessible. What gave me pause wasn't that he was thoughtful, but that he was educated about accessibility and knew what to look for. I attribute that to the ADA creating a general awareness of accessibility issues. The current situation for individuals with disabilities is good, but like anything, it could always be better. As the ADA evolves, it's important for policy makers to be proactive about inclusion of all people with disabilities.

I am lucky to have a family that has helped me when I needed it. But I reflect on others I've met along the way. In El Paso, many families don't speak English. I wonder how their children with disabilities fare. Independent advocates are needed to enforce the ADA. My experience with disability rights has motivated me to pursue a career in disability rights policy. I want to go beyond achieving independence and access for myself—I want to be an advocate for others as well. I am now pursuing a joint graduate degree in Public and Business Administration. My first goal is to work with my university to bring to light accessibility issues, and to participate fully in my commencement ceremonies when I complete my graduate studies. Beyond that, I feel limitless.

Organizations to Contact

The editors have compiled the following list of organizations concerned with the issues debated in this book. The descriptions are derived from materials provided by the organizations. All have publications or information available for interested readers. The list was compiled on the date of publication of the present volume; the information provided here may change. Be aware that many organizations take several weeks or longer to respond to inquiries, so allow as much time as possible.

American Association of People with Disabilities (AAPD)

2013 H Street, NW, Fifth Floor
Washington, DC 20006
(202) 457-0046 or (800) 840-8844 • fax (886) 536-4461
website: www.aapd.com

The American Association of People with Disabilities (AAPD) is the largest disability rights organization in the United States. It is dedicated to ensuring that people with disabilities have equal opportunities, power over their economic situation, the ability to live independently, and the right to participate in the political process. Members are people with disabilities and their families, friends, and supporters. The organization's work focuses on a range of issues, including education, housing, and employment.

The Arc

1825 K Street, NW, Suite 1200
Washington, DC 20006
(202) 534-3700 or (800) 433-5255 • fax (202) 534-3731
email: info@thearc.org
website: www.thearc.org

The Arc, founded in the 1950s, advocates on behalf of individuals with intellectual and developmental disabilities and their families. This community-based organization serves individuals of all ages and can assist with many conditions, including autism, Down syndrome, and fragile X syndrome. The Arc strives to be inclusive, to promote self-determination, and to encourage community integration.

Designing Accessible Communities

15500 Monte Rosa Avenue
Guerneville, CA 95446
(707) 604-7675 or (415) 497-1091 • fax (707) 604-7675
email: richardskaff@designingaccessiblecommunities.org
website: www.designingaccessiblecommunities.org

Designing Accessible Communities is a nonprofit organization that produces educational materials about accessibility for individuals with disabilities and for those who work in the design, construction, and regulation industries. The organization's website provides extensive information on a range of topics related to accessibility, including products and technology, codes and regulations, and policies. It also offers reading lists and links to related websites.

Disability Rights Education and Defense Fund (DREDF)

3075 Adeline Street, Suite 210
Berkeley, CA 94703
(510) 644-2555 • fax (510) 841-8645
email: info@dredf.org
website: www.dredf.org

Disability Rights Education and Defense Fund (DREDF) is a national organization dedicated to the promotion of disability civil rights law and policy. To this end, the organization engages in legal advocacy, training, education, and policy development. Information about specific disability rights issues, such as access to health care, assisted suicide, environmental justice, and disability rights law, are available on its website.

Easter Seals

233 South Wacker Drive, Suite 2400
Chicago, IL 60606
(312) 726-6200 or (800) 221-6827 • fax (312) 726-1494
website: www.easterseals.com

Easter Seals, founded in 1919 as the National Society for Crippled Children, helps individuals with disabilities and their families to deal with the challenges they face, to fulfill their goals, and to live better lives. The organization provides a range of services for children, adults, and seniors, including employment and training, medical rehabilitation, and autism services.

Institute for Human Centered Design (IHCD)

200 Portland Street, Suite 1
Boston, MA 02114
(617) 695-1225 • fax (617) 482-8099
email: info@humancentereddesign.org
website: www.humancentereddesign.org

The Institute for Human Centered Design (IHCD), founded in 1978 as Adaptive Environments, is an international organization that seeks to further design that creates expanded opportunities for individuals of all ages and abilities and to establish a balance between accessibility as required by law and the expansion of best practices in universal, human-centered design. A comprehensive overview of the concept of universal design and a range of publications are available on the IHCD website.

National Council on Independent Living (NCIL)

1710 Rhode Island Avenue, NW, Fifth Floor
Washington, DC 20036
(202) 207-0334 or (877) 525-3400 • fax (202) 207-0341

email: ncil@ncil.org
website: www.ncil.org

The National Council on Independent Living (NCIL), founded in 1982, is a membership organization that promotes independent living and the rights of people with disabilities using consumer-driven advocacy. Its goal is to achieve a world of equal participation for all people. The NCIL website includes a blog, the Advocacy Monitor, which provides current information about the organization's projects and ongoing policy proposals and goals.

National Disability Rights Network (NDRN)

900 Second Street, NE, Suite 211
Washington, DC 20002
(202) 408-9514 • fax (202) 408-9520
email: info@ndrn.org
website: www.ndrn.org

The National Disability Rights Network (NDRN) is a nonprofit membership organization that provides training and technical assistance, legal support, and legislative advocacy to and on behalf of people with disabilities in the United States. The organization is committed to creating a society where equal opportunities and full participation are available to people with disabilities. NDRN advocates for civil rights and attempts to end abuse of people with disabilities.

National Organization on Disability (NOD)

77 Water Street, Suite 204
New York, NY 10005
(646) 505-1191, extension 122 • fax (646) 505-1184
email: info@nod.org
website: www.nod.org

The National Organization on Disability (NOD) is a private, nonprofit organization that seeks to further the complete societal integration of Americans with disabilities. It focuses on advancing employment opportunities and helping to decrease the number of unemployed Americans with disabilities. Detailed information about NOD projects and research is available on the organization's website.

Office of Disability Employment Policy (ODEP)

US Department of Labor, Frances Perkins Building
200 Constitution Avenue
NW Washington, DC 20210
(866) 633-7365
website: www.dol.gov/odep

The Office of Disability Employment Policy (ODEP) is an agency within the US Department of Labor tasked with crafting and evaluating policy to help integrate people with disabilities into the workforce. The agency's work is wide-ranging and includes accommodations, diversity and inclusion, personal assistance services, and veterans' issues. ODEP also manages the website Disability.gov, which offers information about disability programs and services across the country.

World Institute on Disability (WID)

3075 Adeline Street, Suite 280
Berkeley, CA 94703
(510) 225-6400 • fax (510) 225-0477
email: wid@wid.org
website: www.wid.org

The World Institute on Disability (WID), founded in 1983, is an international organization that seeks to achieve full social integration for people with disabilities by increasing employment, economic security, and health care for them. The WID works to achieve this goal through the use of innovative programs and tools, research, training, education, advocacy, and technical assistance.

For Further Reading

Books

James I. Charlton, *Nothing About Us Without Us: Disability Oppression and Empowerment*. Berkeley: University of California Press, 2000.

Ruth Colker, *The Disability Pendulum: The First Decade of the Americans with Disabilities Act*. New York: New York University Press, 2007.

Doris Zames Fleischer and Frieda Zames, *The Disability Rights Movement: From Charity to Confrontation*. Philadelphia, PA: Temple University Press, 2011.

Mary Johnson, *Make Them Go Away: Clint Eastwood, Christopher Reeve and the Case Against Disability Rights*. Louisville, KY: Advocado Press, 2003.

Simi Linton, *Claiming Disability: Knowledge and Identity*. New York: New York University Press, 1998.

Simi Linton, *My Body Politic: A Memoir*, Ann Arbor: University of Michigan Press, 2007.

Paul K. Longmore and Lauri Umanski, eds., *The New Disability History: American Perspectives*. New York: New York University Press, 2001.

Susan Gluck Mezey, *Disabling Interpretations: The Americans with Disabilities Act in Federal Court*. Pittsburgh, PA: University of Pittsburgh Press, 2005.

Jonathan Mooney, *The Short Bus: A Journey Beyond Normal*. New York: Holt, 2008.

Ruth O'Brien, ed., *Voices from the Edge: Narratives About the Americans with Disabilities Act*. New York: Oxford University Press, 2004.

Greg Perry, *Disabling America: The Unintended Consequences of the Government's Protection of the Handicapped*. Nashville, TN: Nelson, 2004.

Joseph P. Shapiro, *No Pity: People with Disabilities Forging a New Civil Rights Movement*. New York: Three Rivers Press, 1994.

Periodicals

Mohammad Ali, Lisa Schur, and Peter Blanck, "What Types of Jobs Do People with Disabilities Want?," *Journal of Occupational Rehabilitation*, June 2011.

Diana Bauer, "The Americans with Disabilities Act Amendments Act," *Business People*, May 2012.

Lorenzo Bowman, "Americans with Disabilities Act as Amended: Principles and Practice," *New Directions for Adult and Continuing Education*, Winter 2011.

Sara Cann, "Disability Assurance," *Fast Company*, December 2012–January 2013.

Tamara C. Daley and Thomas S. Weisner, "'I Speak a Different Dialect': Teen Explanatory Models of Difference and Disability," *Medical Anthropology Quarterly*, March 2003.

Helen Kennedy, Simon Evans, and Siobhan Thomas, "Can the Web Be Made Accessible for People with Intellectual Disabilities?," *Information Society*, January–February 2011.

Scott Lafee, "The Americans with Disabilities Act at 20," *Education Digest*, March 2011.

Jonathan Lazar and Paul Jaeger, "Reducing Barriers to Online Access for People with Disabilities," *Issues in Science and Technology*, Winter 2011.

Paul K. Longmore, "Making Disability an Essential Part of American History," *OAH Magazine of History*, July 2009.

Sara Newman, "Disability and Life Writing: Reports from the Nineteenth-Century Asylum," *Journal of Literary and Cultural Disability Studies*, 2011.

Richard K. Scotch, "'Nothing About Us Without Us': Disability Rights in America," *OAH Magazine of History*, July 2009.

Michelle A. Travis, "Impairment as Protected Status: A New Universality for Disability Rights," *Georgia Law Review*, Summer 2012.

Mark C. Weber, "A New Look at Section 504 and the ADA in Special Education Cases," *Children's Rights Litigation*, 2011.

Paul H. Wehman, "Employment for Persons with Disabilities: Where Are We Now and Where Do We Need to Go?," *Journal of Vocational Rehabilitation*, vol. 35, 2011.

Shirley J. Wilcher, "Broadening the Coverage of the ADA: The 2008 Amendments to the Americans with Disabilities Act," *Insight into Diversity*, November 2010.

Bess Williamson, "Electric Moms and Quad Drivers: People with Disabilities Buying, Making, and Using Technology in Postwar America," *American Studies*, Spring 2012.

Index

A

Accessibility
of activities, 163–164
ADA provisions for, 168–170
for people with disabilities,
170–171
physical access requirements,
10, 151–152, 154
of public transportation, 154,
156
ADA Restoration Act, 27
Advocacy groups, 17–20
See also specific groups
Affirmative action, 144, 146
African American rights, 150
Albertsons, Inc. v. Kirkingburg
(1999), 12
American Coalition of Citizens
with Disabilities (ACCD), 23
American Disabled for Accessible
Public Transit (ADAPT), 25
Americans with Disabilities Act
(ADA)
accessibility and, 168–170
advancing of civil rights,
148–158
amendments to, 13
antidiscrimination provision in,
76–79
attitudes must change, 157–158
extension of rights, 149–151
findings and purpose of, 155
importance of, 166–172
inclusion advances, 171–172
job discrimination limits, 153
overcoming failures in, 152
overview, 149, 167
passing of, 5–6, *19*, 22, 25–27

physical access requirements,
151–152, 154
public transportation access,
154, 156
qualifying for, 12
refuse-to-label message, 105
The Arc (advocacy group), 21
Architectural Barriers Act (1968), 8
Atkins v. Virginia (2002), 13
Autism Rights Watch, 5

B

Barron's Law Dictionary, 130
Baxstrom v. Herold (1966), 62
Behavioral sciences, 65
*Bell v. Wayne County General
Hospital at Eloise* (1974), 58
Bernard, J.L., 56–65
Birnbaum, Morton, 59, 67–68
Bittner, Sascha, 159–165
Blank, Wade, 25
Bolling v. Sharpe (1954), 91
Booth, Edward, 17
Bragdon v. Abbott (1998), 12
Braille menus, 154
Bremer, Jeanne M., 54
Brennan, William J., 117–127, 136
Brooks, William M., 58
Brown, Jerry, 23
Brown, Lester B., 54
Brown v. Board of Education
(1954), 8, 57, 62, 91, 103, 119
Bryce Hospital, 30, *38*
Buck v. Bell (1927), 7
*Burlington School Committee v.
Department of Education* (1985),
11
*Burnham v. Department of Public
Health,* 60

Bush, George H.W., 6, 11–12, 26, 149, *150*
Bush, George W., 13–14, 27

C
Callahan, Josephine, 44
Carter, Jimmy, 24
Center for Independent Living (CIL), 23
Cherry v. Matthews (1976), 24
A Christmas Carol (Dickens), 157–158
Civil Rights Act (1964), 4, 24, 149
Civil Rights Act (1990), 149
Civil rights *vs.* psychiatrists' values, 58
Clark, Kenneth, 62
Cleburne v. Cleburne Living Center (1985), 11
Cleland, Charles C., 41–49
Collins, Clyde Mabry, Jr., 142
Collins, Terri S., 95
Commitment statutes, 58
Committee on Special Education (CSE), 114
Committee on the National Employ the Physically Handicapped Week, 7, 8, 20, 23
Community *vs.* institutional living rights
  ADA protection, 76–79
  eligibility determinations, 82, 84
  of mentally disabled individuals, 75–86
  overview, 76
  quality of life improvements, 80
  segregation as discrimination, 81–82, *105*
  state obligation for community treatment, 86
  state resources and obligations, 79–80, 84–86

Conroy, Terrye, 95
Counseling needs, 112

D
Damascus, Narrel, 70
Dart, Justin, 26
Deaf President Now, 25
Denver independent living center, 25
Department of Health, Education, and Welfare (HEW), 141
Dershowitz, Alan, 62–64, *63*
Developmentally Disabled Assistance and Bill of Rights Act (DDABRA), 35, 81
Dickens, Charles, 157–158
DiPolito, Samantha, 80
Disabilities Education Act (1990), 11–12
Disability, defined, 22, 106–107
Disability Rights Education and Defense Fund, 23, 163
Disability Rights Florida, 5
Disability rights movement
  concept behind, 16–17
  emergence of, 21–23
  expansion of, 20–21
  momentum increases, 23–25
  overview, 15–28
  self-advocacy and, 17, 27–28
Disabled American Veterans (DAV), 18, 20
Disabled children, 4–6, 100–101, 114
  See also Discipline of special needs children
Disabled in Action (DIA), 21
Disabled persons
  accessibility issues, 170–171
  hearing impairments, 152
  physical access requirements for, 10, 151–152, 154

poverty concerns, 102–103
rejection of, 167–168
rights of, 16–17
scoliosis, 113
self-advocacy needs, 17, 27–28
See also Mentally disabled
individuals
Disabled students
evaluation needs, 117–127,
146–147
expulsion of, 130, 132, 135–136
free public education rights,
118–121
suspension of, 130
See also Federally funded education program; Free public
education rights; Integrated
learning environment
Disabled Students' Resident
Program, 164
Discipline of special needs
children
common law principles, 130,
132
difficulties with, *134*
due process in, 133–134
evaluation needs and, 124–126
mandated guidelines for,
128–138
misbehavior and, 132–136
overview, 129–130
parents and experts determination for, 137
policy models for, *131*
purpose of, 137–138
unanswered questions over,
136–137
Discrimination
in access to education, 144, 146
in access to jobs, 19, 25, 153,
156

ADA antidiscrimination provision, 26–27, 76–79, 105, 155
ADA findings on, 155
countering, 5–6, 9, 106
prohibition of, 24, 84, 142
protests against, 21
of school-aged children,
100–101
segregation as, 81–82, *105*
District of Columbia Code, 88–90
Donaldson, Kenneth
abuse and mistreatment, 70–72
feelings of helplessness, 72–73
hope for legal victory, 73–74
overview, 51–52, *52,* 54–55, 67
right to treatment, 67–69
struggle to be released, 66–74, *68*
See also O'Connor v. Donaldson
Due process
in ADA Act, 76
for educational, 11, 122
in Fifth Amendment, 92
in institutional confinement,
57–59
overview, 133–134
violation of, 8, 76, 91–93

E
Education for All Handicapped
Children Act (EHA) (1975), 9,
118, 129, 152
Eighth Amendment, 91
Emergency Relief Bureau, 18
English Speaking Union (ESU),
164
Ennis, Bruce J., 62
Enuresis, 113
Equal employment rights, 18–20
Evaluation needs
court rulings and, 123–124
of disabled students, 117–127,
146–147

Evaluation needs (*continued*)
discipline and, 124–126
IEPs and, 121–122
injunctive relief over, 126–127
overview, 118
right to education and, 118–121
stay-put provision, 122–123
Expulsion of students, 130, 132,
135–136

F
Fair Labor Standards Act (1938), 18
Fair Labor Standards Act (1966),
36
Federally funded education
program
affirmative action not a requisite, 144, 146
auxiliary aids provision,
141–143
denial of admittance to,
139–147
meeting requirements for,
140–141
overview, 139–140
program alteration requirements, 143–144
student evaluation and,
146–147
Fifth Amendment, 91–92
First Amendment, 91
Ford, Gerald, 9, 24
Fourteenth Amendment, 58, 76
Fourth Amendment, 91
Free public education rights
access to, 91–94
cost not an excuse for, 92–93
education plan determination,
94, 96
of mentally disabled individuals, 87–98
overview, 88

parental involvement in education, 95–97
punishment must be limited,
97–98
statute violations, 88–90
student evaluations and,
118–121
Frost, Henry Miles, 4–6

G
Gallaudet University, 25
Ginsberg, Ruth Bader, 75–86, *83*
Goldberg v. Kelly (1969), 93
Goss v. Lopez (1975), 133
Graicunas, V.A., 46
Great Depression, 18
Gross national product (GNP),
153
Gulliver's Travels (Swift), 100

H
Handicapped Children Act (1975),
118
Hatch, Orrin, *19*
Hearing impairments, 152
Heumann, Judy, 21, 23
Hill-Burton Act (1946), 7–8
Hobson v. Hansen (1967), 91–92
Honig v. Doe (1988), 11, *125*, 129–
130, 135–137
Hopkins, Harry, 19
Housekeeping procedures for patients, 39
Hoyer, Steny, *19*
Human Rights Committee, 33
Humane psychological and physical environment, 31–35

I
In re Balley (1973), 63
In-Home Supportive Services provider, 160
Inaccessible activities, 164

Independent Living Centers, 161
Individualized Education Plan
(IEP), 110, 121–122, 132
Individuals with Disabilities
Education Act (IDEA)
accommodation *vs.* differentiation, 106–107
equal education for children,
99–108
harm from classification,
102–104
overview, 21, 27, 100
percentage of time in classroom, *102*
refuse-to-label message,
104–106
separate environments,
100–102
societal changes with, 107–108
Institutional confinement
clarification of terms, 60–64
defining treatment, 64
due process, 57–59
facilities for patients, 37–39
of mentally disabled individuals, 53–55
overview, 57
rates of, *77*
ruling lacks strength, 56–65
treatment guidelines, 59–60
See also Community *vs.* institutional living rights; Minimum
levels of care; Patient care and
rights
Integrated learning environment
defined as an other, 114–115
feelings of guilt and, 113–114
long days and, 112–113
need for, 109–116
overview, 110–111
typical week in, 111–112

*Irving Independent School
District v. Tatro* (1984), 10

J
Jewish European immigrants, 18
Job discrimination, 19, 25, 153,
156
Johnson, Frank Minis, Jr., 29–40,
59–60
Joint Accreditations Commission,
43
Jordan, I. King, 25

K
Katsiyannis, Antonis, 95
Kendall v. True (1975), 63
Kong-Ming, Peter, 44

L
League of the Physically
Handicapped, 18
Least restrictive environment
(LRE) principle, 47
Legal Defense Fund of the
NAACP, 23
Legal Department of the
California Department of
Education, 163
Lennon, John, 100, 102, 108
Leone, Peter E., 137
*Lloyd v. Regional Transportation
Authority* (1977), 10
Long Island University (LIU), 21
Lynch v. Baxley (1974), 58

M
Maintenance procedures for patients, 39
Matthews, F. David, 24
Medication as punishment, 33
Mental health law, 65
Mental Health Systems Act (1980),
35

Mental Retardation Facilities and Community Health Centers Construction Act (1963), 8
Mentally disabled individuals
community *vs.* institutional living rights, 75–86
institutional confinement of, 53–55
institutional confinement ruling lacks strength, 56–65
mental retardation, 152
minimum levels of care, 29–40
right to free public education, 87–98
See also Minimum levels of care; Patient care and rights
Mills v. Board of Education of the District of Columbia (1972), 9, *90*, 103, 119, 123–124
Minimum levels of care
budget conflicts with, 43
could impede institutions, 41–49
effects of growth, 44–46
individualized treatment plans, 40
institution facilities, 37–39
labor must be voluntary, 36
for mentally disabled individuals, 29–40
need for humane environment, 31–35
overview, 29–31, 42–43
personnel cost factors, 44
qualified mental health professionals needed, 32–34, 36, 39–40
rate of growth, 46–49
Multipatient rooms, 37
Murphy v. United Parcel Service (1999), 12

N
Nason v. Superintendent of Bridgewater State Hospital, 57
National Association for Retarded Children (NARC), 21
National Association for Retarded Citizens, 21
National Association for the Advancement of Colored People (NAACP), 23
National Association of the Deaf (NAD), 17
National Center on Law and the Handicapped, 23
National Council on Disability (NCD), 25
National Disability Rights Network, 167
National Federation of the Blind (NFB), 19–20
National Fraternal Society of the Deaf, 18
National Spinal Cord Association, 170
New York Times (newspaper), 67
Nixon, Richard M., 21
No Child Left Behind Act (NCLB), 103, 108, 120
Nonambulatory patients, 39
Nonprofessional staff members, 39

O
O'Brien, Leigh M., 109–116
O'Connor, J.B., 51, 69–71
O'Connor v. Donaldson (1975)
impact of, 57–58
ineffectiveness of, *63*
overview, 60
psychiatrists' values in, 58
treatment, defined, 64
unanswered questions over, 54

See also Donaldson, Kenneth;
  Institutional confinement
Office of Civil Rights, 136–137
Olmsted v. L.C. and E.W. (1999),
  13, 80, 84
Olson, Candy, 4
Oppositional children, 114
Optimum opportunity for treat-
  ment, 37–39

P

PARC v. Pennsylvania (1972), 9,
  103, 119, 123–124
Parental involvement in education,
  95–97
Patient care and rights
  changes to, 35
  institutionalization of mentally
    disabled, 50–55
  right to constitutional liberty,
    51–53, *52*
*Pennsylvania Department of
  Corrections v. Yeskey* (1998), 12
Personal assistance services (PAS)
  accessible activities, 163
  difficulty finding, 160–161
  impact on, 159–165
  inaccessible activities, 164
  overview, 160
  school lack of, 161–163
  transition to independence,
    164–165
Personnel cost factors, 44
Peterson, Beth, 120
PGA Tour, Inc. v. Martin (2001), 13
Physical access requirements, 10,
  151–152, 154
Post-hospitalization plan, 40
Poverty concerns, 102–103
Powell, Lewis F., 139–147, *145*
President's Committee on
  Employment of People with

Disabilities, 153
Professional Golfers' Association
  (PGA), 13
Protection and Advocacy for
  Individuals with Mental Illness
  Act (PAIMI Act) (1998), 35
Public transportation access, 154,
  156

Q

Qualified mental health professional
  patient needs for, 32–34, 36,
    39–40
  posthospitalization plans by, 40

R

Reagan, Ronald, 25
Reeve, Christopher, 170
Refuse-to-label message, 104–106
Rehabilitation Act (1972), 21–22
Rehabilitation Act (1973)
  discrimination and, 142
  interpretation of, 140
  language of, 24, 81, 144
  passage of, 9
  physical access requirements,
    10, 151–152, 154
  veto of, 21–22
  violation of, 137
Religious worship rights of pa-
  tients, 35
Right to constitutional liberty,
  51–53, *52*
Right to education. *See* Free public
  education rights
Roberts, Ed, 22–23
Rolling Quads, 23
Roosevelt, Franklin D., 19
Rouse v. Cameron (1966), 59

S

*Sacramento City School District v.
  Holland* (1994), 12

Scoliosis, 113
Scotch, Richard K., 15–28
Sealed mail rights of patients, 32
Segregation as discrimination, 81–82, *105*
Self-advocacy, 17, 27–28
Sexual rights of patients, 35
Siegel, Ann, 5
Siegel, Loren, 62
Sluyter, Gary V., 41–49
Smith-Sears Veterans Rehabilitation Act, 7
Snowden v. Birmingham-Jefferson County Transit Authority (1977), 10
Southeastern Community College v. Davis (1979), 10
Southern Education Foundation, 167
Special-needs child. *See* Disabled children
Stay-put provision, 122–123
Stewart, Potter, 50–55
Suspension of students, 130
Sutton v. United Airlines (1999), 12
Suzuki v. Quisenberry (1976), 58, 64
Swartz, Jon D., 46
Sweden, 106
Swift, Jonathan, 100

T
Taylor, Steve, 47
Teamsters v. Daniel, (1979), 146
tenBroek, Jacobus, 19–20
Tennessee v. Lane (2004), 13
Thomas, Elwyn, 70, 71
Thornburgh, Dick, 148–158
Treatment
    defined, 64
    guidelines for, 59–60
    individualized treatment plans, 40
    optimum opportunity for, 37–39
    right to treatment, 67–69
    state obligation for community treatment, 86
Tribune (newspaper), 73
Turnbull, Rud, 99–108

U
University of California Berkeley, 22
US Constitution, 88
US Court of Appeals, 133
US Department of Health and Human Services (HHS), 82
US Department of Justice, 81
US Food and Drug Administration, 32

V
Victoria L. v. District School Board (1984), 133–134
Villalobos, Adrian, 166–172, *169*
Visitation rights of patients, 32
Vocational Rehabilitation Amendments, 7

W
Waddy, Joseph Cornelius, 87–98
White Cane Laws, 20
Works Progress Administration (WPA), 18–19
World War I, 18
World War II, 18, 20
Wright, J. Skelly, 91–92
Wyatt v. Stickney (1971), 8, 35, 41, 45, 60, 64

Y
Yell, Mitchell L., 95, 128–138

Z
Zinser, Elizabeth, 25
Zuna, Nina, 99–108